W9-AYN-202

Three Java Dave,
Enjoy the tail!

Delta for Death

Amy Hobbes Newspaper Mysteries, Book

Three

Michele Drier

Michele Drier

Copyright 2015 Michele Drier

All rights reserved. Without limiting the rights under copyright reserved above, no part of this publication may be reproduced, stored in or introduced into a retrieval system, or transmitted, in any form, or by any means (electronic, mechanical, photocopying, recording, or otherwise) without the prior written permission of both the copyright owner and the above publisher of this book.

This is a work of fiction. Names, characters, places, brands, media, and incidents are either the product of the author's imagination or are used fictitiously. The author acknowledges the trademarked status and trademark owners of various products referenced in this work of fiction, which have been used without permission. The publication/use of these trademarks is not authorized, associated with, or sponsored by the trademark owners.

Books by Michele Drier

The Kandesky Vampire Chronicles

Book One, SNAP: The World Unfolds
Book Two, SNAP: New Talent
Book Three, PLAGUE: A Love Story
Book Four, DANUBE: A Tale of Murder
Book Five, SNAP: Love for Blood
Book Six, SNAP: Happily Ever After?
Book Seven, SNAP: White Nights
Book Eight, SNAP: All That Jazz
Book Nine, SNAP: I, Vampire

The Amy Hobbes Newspaper Mysteries

Edited for Death
Labeled for Death
Delta for Death

Dedication

For Illa Collin, stalwart

CHAPTER ONE

I have to get out of here.

Shimmers of heat rise off the parking lot behind the Monroe *Press*. If I squint the right way, I can pretend it's a mirage on the Sahara west of the Nile, or at least the Mojave outside of Palm Springs. I'm tiring of living in the Central Valley and a change looks good now.

Any change.

I know the urge for change is an omen for this summer.

It's the last week in May and we've already had two days of temperatures more than 105. We don't hit "triple digits" as the TV people say until the last of June as a rule. This year will be different.

Is it global warming? Who knows? Personally I think so, but I've only been on this planet a tad over forty years, not enough to fully witness or understand earth cycles that take millennia.

What I can do is head into the newsroom, grab a reporter or two and assign them to do a weather story. Heat, wind, rain, storms, it's all fodder for the *Press*, a paper that every day brings news to people in Monroe—and a few surrounding small towns and areas.

I'm Amy Hobbes, the managing editor, a job that I fell into when my ex-husband moved to Illinois with his pregnant girlfriend, leaving me and my then-high-school aged daughter to cope alone. We've coped pretty well. I kept my house, my daughter is set to graduate from UC Santa Barbara with a nursing degree and has a job lined up as an ER trauma nurse at the UC Davis hospital in Sacramento.

I'm not sure why wanderlust hit this morning. Maybe it's a holdover from the adrenaline rush of being a reporter on a breaking news story, a rush I only get vicariously now.

Once out of the sun, my eyes take a second to adjust from the glare. I take a deep breath and fan myself with the paper I picked up in the backshop, where the final layout of the *Press* gets checked. It's cooler in the newsroom and I call Gwen and Sally into my office for a chat.

"We need a heat story."

They're both veterans who've chosen to stay in Monroe and at the *Press* for the duration. This isn't a new story for them, so the eyerolls are at a minimum.

"There are some soccer leagues forming." Sally is the education writer and has a handle on all things youth-related. "I'll talk to a coach and some parents about keeping kids cool and hydrated during practice." She hesitates. "Then again, if any of them make it to the World Cup, they'll be playing in the summer. Maybe this is good conditioning." She smiles as she heads for her phone.

Sometimes print reporters have an edge over broadcast. While the TV reporter is out in the heat, rain, wind, wearing hipboots in a flood or a parka in the snow, newspaper reporters are usually on the phone. Their "eyewitness" descriptions most times mean they stuck their head out the door.

Then again, the pay stinks.

Gwen is quiet. She's the city hall reporter and tuned into local politics as well as some state issues that affect our small spot on the map.

"We've done it and done it, but another story on water use and probable rationing wouldn't hurt. It just kills me to watch sprinklers running for hours in this heat. What do they think they're going to drink or flush their toilets or shower with this year?"

She's hit on the elephant. California is in the midst of a serious drought. It's so serious that CalTrans has messages on their freeway signs "Severe drought, conserve water," although what anyone can do zipping by at seventy-five is beyond me.

I know, I know, it's a way to keep the issue on everyone's mind, but installing water meters might help. Odd as it sounds, there's a huge swath of the Central Valley, including such cities as Fresno and Sacramento, that didn't have meters installed. They're coming.

Water is always a huge issue in this state. With more than three-quarters of the population living south of the Tehachapi Mountains in Southern California—an area that's semi-arid at best—and less than a few hundred thousand living in the rain-drenched northern coastal areas, it's a classic case of the haves and the have-nots. And there are *way* more have-nots in this battle.

There's currently a proposal to build huge tunnels under the Delta—the confluences of the Sacramento, American and San Joaquin rivers that empty into San Francisco Bay—and ship water from the Sacramento River south. This pits north against south as nothing else can. In Northern California, the stereotype is Southern Californians lolling around their pools while the north is drained dry.

In fact, most of the water in California is consumed by the huge agribusinesses in the Central Valley. Rice, almonds, cotton. And ag is such an economic engine that its lobbyists get heard.

I haven't formed a hard opinion on the tunnel issue and have a meeting scheduled with some folks from Water Resources in Sacramento later this week. I'll need to pick a position and write an editorial before the fall election.

This isn't getting a heat story done. I message Luis, my photographer, to go down to a river beach—any river, any beach—and shoot kids and boaters.

Then I send a note to Clarice, my cops reporter, to see me. I'll have her do a story on the cops and firefighters who do water rescues during the summer. There are always some young male idiots who take a case or two of beer out on their ski boat, leave the lifejackets behind (more room for the beer) and run into trouble.

Who'd think it?

As I reach for my phone, it rings with Clarice's number. "Do you have something?"

"I do. It'll be a nice small story on the inside local page."

What? Clarice isn't pushing for page one? It must be small.

"What is it?"

"It's a nice weird, quirky murder."

Only Clarice could call a murder story nice, small and quirky.

"So tell."

I hear her suck in a breath. "Well, the Monroe cops went to serve a warrant on one of our local druggies and thought he was acting strange. Two of his pals were sitting on a couch in the living room, kinda smushed together. Then the cops notice a strange odor and a dark liquid oozing out from under the couch. They think it might be meth chemicals and since the warrant is drug-related, ask if they can come in. They ask the pals to move, see the couch is the hide-a-bed kind, start to pull open and out rolls a body."

"You're kidding! They stuffed a body in a couch and then sat on it as a cover-up? Our bad guys are slipping."

I hear some background yelling on the phone, then Clarice says, "Better go, they're booking three guys now. Not sure who did what to whom yet so all are getting murder charges."

The phone goes dead in my hand.

CHAPTER TWO

I mull over Clarice's latest murder. Some days a drug deal gone bad is just more of the usual. This might be part of the reason for my escape dreams.

Over the weekend, I took my little red sports car out for a drive through the Delta.

When the heat's up, it's usually cooler along the rivers than in the mountain Gold Rush towns, but both have spiffy, curvy roads for driving. Of course, the Delta roads are on the tops of the levees, so one side drops off to farmland and the other goes straight into the Sacramento River. Several cars are pulled out every year, some with bodies, some without.

I don't push for speed on these drives, but for interest. So much of my driving is freeway, up and down the flat valley, that it's a challenge to see if I still remember how to take the curves on these narrow roads. This weekend, I did a couple of detours into some tiny towns like Walnut Grove and Courtland. A lot of small-scale farmers are here, making a living for generations from the rich alluvial soil washed down from the Sierra Nevada, forming islands that flooded in the spring. Levees were built by Chinese laborers beginning in the 1850s to drain the wetlands and keep the rivers in their beds.

As a child, I'd go with my mother to visit relatives. She'd drive these roads from San Francisco to the valley and it was a scary thrill to ride along at the level of the tree tops. During the spring, there'd usually be at least one fire in the peaty soil where asparagus was grown, and I'd wonder why the land would be smoking. "They can't put the fire out," my mother would say. "It's down in the ground. They just have to wait until it burns itself out."

Occasionally I had nightmares about being lost in the soft, fire-eaten landscape, following the smoke that drifted up from under the ground.

Now, I'm more interested in all the tidy yards in the small towns that sport "Stop the Tunnels" signs. I noted a few addresses that I'll look up in the reverse-directory. Call the owners and talk to them about their opposition.

On the surface, it looks like a classic David and Goliath fight. The pro-tunnel forces are underwritten by two of the state's largest water retailers, the Metropolitan Water District in Los Angeles and the Westland Water District, headquartered in Fresno. Together, they take more than fifty-five percent of the water currently exported from the Delta.

Lined up against them are the small farmers and residents in the Delta, fish and wildlife groups, The Sierra Club, Friends of the River, the Bay-Delta Conservancy Group and environmentalists throughout the state.

What the anti forces have on their side is the battle over the Peripheral Canal, a project that skirted around the Delta, taking Sacramento River water south. An idea defeated by voters in 1982.

That drive took me through bucolic areas of fields, by small marinas and on a one-lane road along a barely-moving slough of green water, overhung with trees making a tunnel of shade across the pavement. I had the top down, the day was hot and I pushed against the urge to pull over and nap in the coolness.

I did pull over when my phone rang. It was Phil, a friend who works for the San Francisco *Times* and is quickly becoming a Person of Interest in my personal life. He wants to know if I'd like to spend next weekend with him in the city, taking in a museum or two—and whatever else came up.

Maybe this invitation is what set off my wanderlust this morning. I'm always up for a day or two in San Francisco and Phil is getting to be the icing on the cake.

I'm dragged out of my reverie when Clarice barrels into my office, bringing a wave of heat with her. She's a big-boned blond, brash, bullying, opinionated and my best reporter. I've asked, well maybe threatened, to take her off the cops beat and put her on some higher visibility beat but she fights me every time. She fell in love with Pulitzer Prize-winning Edna Buchanan of the Miami *Herald* in J-school and takes on the cops beat every day with a joy of discovery that's hard to argue with.

"So, who gets charged with murder?"

She gives me an odd look, fanning herself with her notebook, which causes pens, paperclips and scraps of notes to flutter out like cherry blossoms in spring.

"What murder?" she asks with a display of innocence a defense lawyer would love.

"You know, the body stuffed in the hide-a-bed. The one you called me about."

"Oh, that." She huffs out a breath to unstick her sweaty bangs from her forehead. "They charged all three of them with murder, but two will probably plead down to accessory. It's just a low-brow drug deal gone bad. The victim," she flips through notebook pages, causing more fallout, "is Lester 'Lace' Freeman who has—well had—a long sheet of run-ins, almost all possession or possession with intent to sell. Personally, I think he tried to stiff the other guys out of money."

She looks up and grins. "It didn't help that all of them were higher than flying pigs. Crack, I'm thinking. The tox screens on Freeman will take a while. The other three gave at the jail."

"Well, how long are you planning to write?" I need to get an estimate of the length so I can work with the desk on placing the story.

"I think six inches for an inside local page."

If Clarice isn't pushing for a longer story, and page one play, she really doesn't think this is spectacular. There's a chance that they'll all plea bargain and end up with several years in prison, simply adding to the overpopulation.

I look at her. I'm trying to frame a story about jails and prisons stuffed to the gills. This means there are some number of prisoners who get early paroles and are back on the streets, which makes a lot of cops and prosecutors see red, but as I'm mulling this over, she raises a finger.

"But," she says. "But, I have a tip on something much better."

A better murder?

CHAPTER THREE

"**I** just happened to be outside Jim Dodson's office and overheard something about a possible body in one of the corporation yards out on the Delta."

OK, this sentence needs several questions.

"What were you doing outside *Sheriff* Dodson's office? The couch murder was in the city cops jurisdiction. And where in the Delta? That's got a lot of jurisdictional overlap and may not even be ours to cover."

I know that Clarice and Jim Dodson are an item. I know they've been seeing each other for a few months. I've told Clarice to be very careful about involvement with anyone from law enforcement...it can taint her objectivity and possibly break her heart. And I've told her repeatedly to use his title in all work-related conversations, particularly here at the *Press* or at the Sherriff's department.

She hears my reprimand and gets more pink than simply the heat can justify. "Sorry, Amy. I ran by his office to see if he wanted to get a drink after work. I'm careful. If he has anyone in his office, or his door is closed, I don't even stop. Today, there were a couple deputies in the hallway talking about going out to the Delta. It felt to me like the tip wasn't very solid."

I'm bashing around in my brain trying to place the corporation yard. The tunnels, and any work on them, haven't begun...and probably won't for a few years. First is the cost—estimates run from $25 billion in initial construction bonds to $67 billion by the time the bonds are paid off. That's billion, with a B. Certainly the state is huge—Chamber of Commerce types like to talk about California having the eighth largest economy in the world—but $50 or so billion is a big chunk of change.

Then there's the backlash from the Stop The Tunnels crowd.

Ah, now I remember a small cyclone-fenced yard near the little spot called Freeland. To date, the town's claim to fame has been a couple of Delta drinking establishments. Fistfights but not a hotbed of dead bodies.

"Are you talking about the fenced area near Freeland? Is that what you're calling the corporation yard?"

"I think so. There isn't anything else out there that's storing heavy equipment."

"Since this is all jumping the gun, who has equipment out there? They haven't started anything."

"Well, they haven't begun, but what they're planning to do is drill a series of core samples to map a route for the tunnels."

"That sounds a little innocuous."

She nods her head in agreement. "Doesn't seem like anything to get killed over, which is why the deputies aren't sure it's a solid tip."

"Talk to me about the drilling. We haven't done a story on this yet. When did they move the equipment in? When are they planning to begin?"

Her eyes drift up to the ceiling. Is there an answer painted on the tiles there? In the silence, I wander into a dead-end of wondering whether there's asbestos in those tiles...just like in the schools I went to as a kid.

Clarice snaps me back with, "I'm pretty sure we ran a brief from Sacramento when they announced the drilling. It was supposed to start last month."

"'Supposed' to start? Has it or hasn't it?"

"No, it hasn't. I need to find out what's slowing it down."

"Wait a minute. Since when are you the state government reporter?"

She purses her lips and gives me The Glare. If she didn't amuse me and consistently turn in good, well-written stories, I might slap her with insubordination when that look hits. As it is, I glare right back.

"Amy," she says in her teen put-upon voice, "don't you think I need to do background if the tip on a body turns out?"

I stare at her. She's knitting a theory together out of invisible yarn and I suspect she sees a complete sweater while I'm looking at air.

"Just check out the body tip first. If there is one, and you think the cops can tie it to the tunnels or drilling or any other of the big plans for the Delta then it may be time to dig into the drilling."

A smirk wisps across her face so fast I'm not sure I really see it.

"'Dig' into the drilling?"

"Go. Go find a body. Go work on the water rescue team story. I'd have thought the visual of cops and firefighters in swim gear or wetsuits would have you intrigued."

Clarice nods, a speculative look in her eye. "Some of them are easy to watch."

She sighs, then, "The story is almost finished, just need to assign some photos. I thought I could do a sidebar on the drought luring people to the rivers. We may have low water in the reservoirs but the rivers are still running."

"Good." I put Clarice's swift water rescue and sidebar with art into the story budget for the weekend and glance at her as she strolls to her desk. She has something in her mind, she gave up too easily on the Delta tip. There isn't anything I can do until we have some confirmation so I pull the city council agenda up. The council finally has the change in zoning request for the mega-church, Harvest of Praise, on the agenda for tomorrow night and there's bound to be a crowd. I message Gwen and Luis to say we'll hold page one for a late story and cc the copydesk on the message.

Either way the vote goes, probably half the town is going to be angry. I write a note for Clarice to ask the city police if they're adding officers to the night shift for the meeting. Long shot, this is a peaceable small city but with the heat, you never know. It's just zoning for a church, after all.

The coming weekend with Phil is taking up a chunk of my mind. The invitation was casual, take in a museum or two and whatever else came up. I was happy that we'd reached a point in our relationship...or dating or whatever we might call our hanging out...that we didn't need to have a specific agenda.

Because Phil and I were friends and co-workers almost twenty years ago in the San Fernando Valley, we have an ease with each other. We'd never gotten together romantically. One or the other of us was involved with someone when the other was free so when he moved to San Francisco and I was in Monroe, both single, seeing each other just seemed a natural progression.

He's a good friend, a bright, quick, articulate man who's the art critic for the San Francisco *Times*. This critic gig is just the most recent area for him. He's a Quebecois, fluent in French, a dabbler in various genres of art with a scholarly book out on the extent of Gothic Revival architecture in North America. One of the chapters is on Grace Cathedral in San Francisco, the seat of the Episcopalian Diocese of

California. I secretly think he fell in love with the building, which was a moving force in getting him to leave SoCal.

We have great times together, but I wonder if that's because we live roughly a hundred miles apart and only spend a few days together at a time. We both have control issues that could crop up if we got too comfortable with each other.

For now, I'm happy hanging out and absorbing his sometimes weird and esoteric knowledge about things...art, architecture, wine, history, great food and race cars. He owns a vintage Porsche and loves to drive it, hard, on the same twisty, turny roads that appeal to me.

And it's Phil who's given me back my trust and lust for men after Brandon left me high and dry. Phil's helped me discover a sexy side that had been buried in the daily push for survival as a single mom.

I'm drifting down a path of daydreams when my cell launches into "Who Let the Dogs Out", the ring I'd programmed in for Clarice, sure that it was loud enough to get my attention.

It was and it does and I say, "Talk to me."

"Yep, there's a body."

"Probably a lot of bodies, all in all. Care to tell me where, what, who...you know the drill."

Clarice huffs. She gets testy if I bring her back to reality when she's in her Dick Tracy or Joe Friday persona.

"They did find a body at the corporation yard near Freeland. Male, about fifty, no ID yet. It's going to be in Sheriff Dodson's jurisdiction for now, unless the CHP steps in because it's a state work area. None of the sheriff's detectives would let me get close, they'd already done the scene forensics and had him in a body bag before they'd talk to me."

From her tone of voice, Clarice is not pleased. And when Clarice is unhappy, lots of people around her can get unhappy, fast.

CHAPTER FOUR

There isn't enough information to write anything but a brief for tomorrow's edition, which makes Clarice even more grumpy. But knowing Clarice, she'll be at Jim Dodson's side until he releases some of the W's.

She heads out, hoping to catch the Sheriff for a drink and I head home to Mac.

The house is stuffy. I won't leave doors or windows open in this heat, but I do leave the air set at seventy-eight so Mac has some relief. From the piles of black dog hair in the foyer, I can tell he's spent most of the day lying on the tile floor, but he's right at the laundry room door to meet me as I come in from the garage. He's jumping around, I check his empty water bowl and shoo him out the back sliding glass door. He was hard to house train, but now seldom has accidents and the few he's had have been on the floor of my shower.

I kick off my sandals, strip my sodden shirt, skirt and underwear off and leave them in a pile, wrap a bath sheet around me and head for the pool. Skinny-dipping in the evening after a hot day cools me faster than dropping the thermostat, but I'll have to do that later in order to sleep.

Mac runs along beside me as I do a couple of languid laps. This isn't for exercise. I climb out, towel-dry enough to pull on some fresh clothes and head for the kitchen. Grazing in the refrigerator and freezer wipes the last of the day's heat off and there's some left-over chicken salad that I can wrap in a lettuce leaf. I'm just finishing up when Heather calls. Her graduation is in a month and there are "arrangements," one of which is whether or not I'll come down for it.

"Mom, I love you, but it's just going to be a madhouse." Like many other colleges and universities, UCSB has gone to a mass ceremony. Not even those getting PhDs are called by name, let alone walk across the stage. And a lowly BS in nursing gets to stand up with the rest of the School of Science...about fifteen hundred strong. "I don't even think you'll be able to see me!"

She's right, and logic would have me running the other way, but she's my baby. She's worked hard to get to this place and I'm fantastically proud of her. I suspect she doesn't want me there because she thinks I'll cry...and I probably will.

"I know, but I still want to see you. Take you out to lunch or dinner. I can even help you move."

"Bwwwahhh...," her laugh of derision echoes. "Are you planning to help by loading up your car? My shoes might fit."

"I was thinking more along the lines of packing, Missy." Yeah, my Miata won't make a good van.

"I've already started some packing. Well, more like weeding through my books and clothes. I want to have it all done at least two days before graduation. Everything I'll need for those last two days is going in my suitcases."

This is *my* daughter talking? When did she grow up and start to plan ahead? "I'm impressed. When are you going to look for a place to live?"

There are voices in the background and Heather sounds like she's drinking. "Are you guys partying?"

"Hardly. We're drinking coffee and pulling a study session. I'm coming up in a couple of weeks to find a place. I start work with my preceptor a week after graduation."

There's a silence at her end, then she clears her throat. "Um…hmmm. I was hoping that you could loan me the money for first, last and a deposit. I'm thinking of looking at some of the older apartments in midtown. Living in the student ghetto has been fun, but I'll be working nights and I'm ready for a quieter place."

"Of course I will. And that's a nice neighborhood. I'll have your room ready and we can have a lunch and some shopping."

"Don't cram too much in, Mom. I just want to find a place and spend some lounging pool time before I head back for the last finals. By the way, if I'm there will it cramp your style with Phil? How's that going?"

So, one of the downsides of a grown-up daughter. "No, you're not cramping my style. I'm going to San Francisco this weekend and that will be a Phil fix for a bit. It's not totally your business, but things are going fine."

I hear a chuff of amusement then she says, "Alright, I don't want TMI. I love you and see you weekend after this. If you're bound on coming down for the ceremony, we'll put you up on a futon for a couple of nights. Jen is staying here this summer, so she'll be looking for roommates but she's waiting until after graduation."

By the time we say our "I love yous," it's cooled enough to take Mac out for his evening stroll and meet-and-greet. He and the Schnauzers three blocks away have a love-hate relationship, but after he stayed with them for a day while I was in the hospital, it's way more friendly. They all bark, but now there's more sniffing.

Home, I flip on CNN for background drone as I start a search on "drilling and core samples." Lord, there's ice, mud, soil, trees, rocks...it seems as though every place on earth is being forced to give up its history through scientists dissecting a six-inch diameter column of stuff. Much of it hasn't seen the light of day for hundreds, thousands, maybe millions of years.

I'm just going off on a tangential search for tree-ring dating when Phil calls.

"Do you have company? I hope I'm not interrupting."

"No, it's just the TV. How are you?" I can feel my voice slowing and deepening. Dang, I'm not even consciously doing that. It always amazes me when my body takes over from my mind and being around Phil brings on that reaction...in spades.

"I'm fine, looking forward to this weekend. Have you thought about anything you'd like to do?"

Some images flash through my mind, not things I want to share in a phone conversation. "Hmmm...not really. Just getting out of the heat for a couple of days will be good. Maybe a drive down the coast?"

"You've got it. What's your calendar for the next few weekends?"

"Weekend after next Heather's coming up to look for an apartment; two weeks after that, I'm going down for her graduation. Wonder of wonders, she seems to have the move itself under control." Phil's met Heather a few times, lately at hospitals when I've ended up in the ER. She hasn't shone in those stress situations, but maybe my "accident" history had something to do with her choosing nursing as a career.

"You know I'm not much of a joiner...or maybe you didn't know...but in L.A. I joined the Porsche Owner's Club. Never did a lot with them, but I ran across their schedule and in three weeks they're holding time trials at Laguna Seca. Would you want to go?"

A weekend with Phil? In Monterey? With sports cars? Hard duty, but someone has to take it. And I did. "I'd love to!"

Two weekends with Phil and two with Heather. Even my June calendar is heating up.

CHAPTER FIVE

I'm typing some notes and links on core samples for Clarice when Rafe calls. He's one of the town's self-appointed overseers, busy-bodies and newshounds who occasionally has a decent tip. Today, he's telling me that the acreage where Harvest of Praise, the new mega-church, is going in has a line of picketers.

"They're waving placards and shouting," he says.

"Who's 'they,' Rafe?"

"All the folks who tried to stop the church zoning."

As news-tips go, this is about a two until he says, "They have a bunch of signs that say 'I'm a NIMBY and proud of it'."

That's a little out of the ordinary. Almost all construction sites get a contingent of "not in my back yards" but not many of them are so brazen as to say they're proud of it.

"I'll send someone to check it out. Thanks for calling." I've found with Rafe that it's good to make the conversations short and to the point. I don't know if he goes as far as seeing hovering black helicopters but he certainly has an oar in the conspiracy galley.

A note to Don Roberts with a cc to Gwen nets me a bottle of whine standing in my office door.

"Why should I have to go out there?" Roberts is definitely one of those who wants to cover a story while sitting at his desk.

"Because you're the religion reporter. Aren't you the least bit interested in why people in the neighborhood don't want a church?"

"Well, they've said they don't want the noise and traffic." He's not giving up easily.

"OK, why did the council approval last night change things? Why are they out today in this heat protesting a done deal? Go and ask some of them."

Roberts starts to open his mouth then catches my look, closes it, snails to his desk, picks up a notebook and. with a sigh deep enough to collapse a lung, heads out the door.

Gwen and Luis, the photographer, are in line behind him and they both do an eye roll at his attempt to shirk work. I nod at both of them. "Luis, get some good pictures. It's a church versus a neighborhood. There're bound to be some kids dragged out by their mommies. Gwen, get a quote from somebody at the city. Planning director, City Attorney, Manager if you can get him."

Last night's council vote was perfunctory. This issue had seen several public meetings, contentious planning meetings and threatened lawsuits on both sides, so the final vote, even though the chambers were packed, was anti-climatic. I send a quick email to Clarice to check the cops log for possible disturbances but don't expect anything.

She's all bustle when she shows up—dropping her purse, phone, notebook, keys, sunglasses on her desk and bee-lining for my door.

"I stopped by to talk to *Sheriff* Dodson this morning."

"And? Did you find out anything new?"

"Not last night. He was too busy to go for a drink. This morning, a little. The dead guy is Johnson Byers. He was an employee of Earth/Search, one of the companies the state subcontracted some of the sampling work to. He was an equipment operator, ran the machine that drilled the hole for the core. He and his crew had been out yesterday and got a couple of cores. Died from blunt trauma to the head. They wouldn't tell me what, but there are big, heavy tools, pipes, pieces of metal all over the place out there."

"So what now?"

She shakes her head. "I haven't a clue. I'll call his family, track down his friends and neighbors, but he lived outside of Sacramento so I don't want to spend too much time on it."

Something's got her stirred up, I can tell. Her forehead is furrowed and her eyelids are at half-mast. "Spill. What has you spooked."

"I'm not spooked, I just can't figure why this guy ended up a victim." Then her eyes get wide. "Wait a minute. What if this has nothing to do with the guy's work? Maybe he was a gambler and owes money? Naw, they'd probably shoot him. But what if he was having an affair? Bashing in the head is more of a crime of the moment...using anything handy as a weapon."

"Come back, Clarice. Have you been watching those true crime TV series again?"

She focuses. "Alright, alright. Just idle speculation. I don't think the cops have any more ideas than I do."

She's covered the cops beat long enough that she can probably outline an investigation better than some of the rookies, but I constantly try to keep her reined in. It doesn't do to get the cops—any of the cops, they all talk to each other—angry at you.

"Have they, or you, thought about the anti-tunnel crowd? It's gotta be difficult to work every day in the middle of signs that tell you to go away."

She gives me a look that seems to wonder if the heat has fried my brain. "Yes, Amy," patience drips like a slow IV. "I asked *Sheriff* Dodson about that and he said they're canvassing the neighborhood now."

I snap my fingers as a sudden scene pops in my head. "You know, last weekend when I was out there, I jotted down some street addresses of folks who had Stop the Tunnels signs in their yard. Why don't you go out and see some of them? You can always use them in one of the next tunnel stories. And in the meantime, what do they feel about having someone murdered practically in their back yard?"

Her face lights up a little. I'm sure a day hanging in the cooler air of the Delta is appealing with the valley heat.

"Sounds good, and speaking of back yards, the NIMBY picketing crew hasn't caused any problems yet. The city cops sent one traffic officer out to monitor it. Buncha soreheads. 'I got mine, too bad for you.' Those people make me crazy. I'd love to see their toys get taken away."

I'm supposed to be impartial, but I agree with Clarice. The other ones who make me cranky are the urbanites escaping to the little towns in the foothills for their "small-town charm." In a couple of years, they start to lobby for bringing in big-box and upscale stores for shopping ease. The entry streets to a lot of the growing mountain towns are lined with chain grocery and home improvement stores, eclipsing the charm and driving local, small stores out of business.

Clarice shrugs. "At least most of the towns in the Delta have stayed untouched. Maybe it's because the farmers haven't sold land to developers."

She may be right. The land in the Delta has been ag since the first levees were built by Chinese laborers in the eighteen-sixties. Several of the farms are now in the hands of the fourth or fifth generation.

There's another piece of this, though and that's the levees themselves. They're on some of the "most endangered" list of infrastructure in the country but the state and federal governments haven't moved them up to a high enough priority to start repairs.

Which makes ag the only sensible use for the land that could flood when a levee ruptures.

California...water is always contentious.

CHAPTER SIX

With Clarice out in the Delta, things are quiet. Two people are busy at their keyboards, one on the phone, others at meetings or interviews. I take advantage of the after-lunch lull to get my nails done.

Phil and I have been friends long enough that I don't over-primp for him, but I want to be professional and prepared if I meet any of his urban contemporaries. I leave my holey t-shirts and ratty walk-the-dog shorts at home when I go to visit. This time, a decent manicure as well.

Walking into the nail salon is always an altered universe. The workers are Vietnamese and the space is full of chatter. Noise and voices that I don't have to pay any attention to, just let the unfamiliar language bathe me in a stream of voices who don't want anything from me.

I use this time to let my mind wander. Every so often an honest and interesting idea swims by, like the time I wondered about the practice of a rural vet. It netted a light, wry piece about a woman who gave up helping the dogs, cats and birds...and an occasional lizard...and tooled around the back roads in her huge four-wheel-drive truck, taking on patients several times her size.

Today I'm free-wheeling in idle when a voice says, "I wouldn't put it past him to bash someone's head in."

I glance at the mirrors lining the walls to spot the conversation and see two women engrossed with each other, not paying any attention to their surroundings. Perfect set-up for eavesdropping. I snap out of my trance and listen.

Woman One, a fifty-something heavy-set brunette is nodding. "He's always had a short fuse. I thought he'd beat on Suzy when she let that surveyor into their backyard."

"I know," says Woman Two, a blond a few years older than her friend but trying to fight the battle of the lines. Her forehead doesn't wrinkle, probably from her Botox treatments.

Both of them are dressed in jeans and shirts but these look like they've been put on for work, not for show. I peg them as farmers' wives, come into the big town of Monroe for an afternoon of beauty and shopping. Come in from where, though? Surveyors are a common sight around Madison County...checking lot lines for developments, laying out new vineyards, sighting for road improvements. Except not many of these take place in someone's back yard.

Taking care not to slide sideways out of the chair, I lean slightly to listen. They chat on, their voices lowered when they talk about Suzy. The consensus is that Suzy's a battered woman, not ready to pull the plug on the relationship. The friends are disgusted but stick by her. Interesting, dreadful, heart-wrenching, not a story, though.

As they begin gathering their things to go, I brazen into their conversation. "You guys look like you're staying cool in this heat." Not in the top ten of interruptions, just enough to get a foot in.

Woman Two pats her hair. "It's OK. We always hate coming into town. The temperature is usually higher here than at home."

"Really? Where's home? I may have to move there."

"Oh, honey, you wouldn't like it there. Used to be nice, but it's being ruined now with all the tourists." Woman One nods in agreement. Hmmm...probably the foothills, then.

Just as I'm losing interest, Woman Two says, "And it's only going to get worse if those damned tunnels go in. We won't have any water left for irrigation. Four generations of our family, poof, gone, up in dust."

The Delta. With a brief thought that I'm going to Purgatory I say, "I didn't mean to eavesdrop," quick look in the mirror for nose length, "but I was upset when I heard about Suzy." I shake my head. "I'm with the Monroe *Press* and it just tears my heart out to hear stories about domestic abuse. Do you think she'll get out?"

"Not likely." Woman One tugs her bag up on her shoulder and tilts her head at the door. This little interview is over. Funny how a mention of the press can kill a perfectly normal gossip.

"Well, I hope Suzy's safe, and you're cooler at home." I wave one wet hand at them as they crowd each other out the door.

That expedition didn't net anything solid. Farmers in the Delta upset at the tunnels proposal, and Suzy, a battered wife who's choosing to stay with her husband, a batterer with a short fuse. What did one of the women say? She wouldn't put it past him to bash someone's head in?

My nails aren't quite dry. They'll set in this heat, I just have to be careful about typing for the next hour or so. Time for a phone conversation with Clarice.

When she answers, I hear road noise over the rock pouring out of her car stereo. "Pull over," I yell.

"Let me get to a spot where I can," then several seconds of silence from Clarice and the sound of a car engine turning off. Stereo still blasting.

"Clar," I shout, knowing full well she can hear me, I just can't hear her. "Jeez, alright," she says, the volume goes down and my brain stops vibrating.

"Why did you answer if you were driving?"

"Because the company I work for is too cheap to get me a hands-free? Because if I let you go to voicemail, I'd get ripped for not answering? Any other reasons you want to choose from?"

I grit my teeth. Both she and I need to have hands-free devices, but Calvin and Max, the publishers, think them an unnecessary expense. If we need to talk, we can just pull over because they won't pay a ticket for using a cell phone, either. Buying them, though, will also frost relations with the other reporters who won't get hands-frees. I really pushed the expense envelop when I managed to wangle cell phones for them. We're on the basic plan with the least minutes and if anyone runs over, I'm the one who gets to scrutinize the bills each month and make them pony up for non-business calls. A scenario no one likes or wants.

"We can take the cell phone complaints up later. I just had my nails done..." I hear a snicker. "This is good. There were two women, farmers' wives from the Delta in the salon, too, and they were having a conversation about some guy who beats his wife."

"You made me stop in a pullout along the levee for that?" Disgust is dripping.

"Watch it. I can still put you on a features beat. One woman said, 'I wouldn't put it past him to bash somebody in the head,' then they thought he might have beaten Suzy because she let a surveyor into their back yard."

In the silence, I hear a few cars swishing by on the narrow road. "Are you there?"

"I'm here, Amy. Do you have any names beside 'Suzy'? It's probably worth a few questions but I don't know where to start."

I blow a breath out. "When you get back, take a look at the calls log in the sheriff's department. The way these two women were talking, beating Suzy is one of her husband's routine occupations. Somebody had to have called in a domestic disturbance."

CHAPTER SEVEN

I'm in Sacramento, meeting with the Public Information Officer from Water Resources. I've seen pictures of the devastation caused by the drought in the southern reaches of the Central Valley, and am gobsmacked at pictures of Lake Oroville, in the north.

Oroville Dam is the tallest dam in the United States and holds the second largest reservoir in California. The huge Northern California lakes of Shasta and Oroville are only at about thirty percent of capacity, less than half of their historic averages. The edges are marked with hundreds of feet of brown dirt, a visual reminder of how far the levels have dropped.

Will the tunnels project have any impact on the states' drought conditions in the future? Well, it seems to depend on who you ask and I need to get the arguments for both sides before I can take an editorial stand.

Hans, a hydraulic engineer and the PIO for the department, leans back in his chair. His office walls are papered with maps showing the paths of water movement through the state. Dark blue lines are rivers, lighter blue lines are state water projects—canals that shoot irrigation water south to the thirsty Central Valley ag lands—green are the federal water projects—more canals—and yellow are the pumping stations. Separate maps show the smaller reclamation and irrigation districts. The maps are a spider web overlay of California.

"You want to talk about the tunnel project?" He moves around to the front of his desk and leans a hip on the corner. This guy is a master at putting people, and the press, at ease. He exudes a friendly let's-just-chat attitude and I pull out a notebook, cross my legs and settle in for a talk.

"I'm going to have to write an editorial about the tunnel project, and we have a lot of readers in and around the Delta. There are tons of small farmers, uh, families with small farms, out there who are pretty upset about this proposal."

Hans nods. "This isn't a popular proposal...at least in this part of the state. There's a feeling that it's 'our' water because the rain falls here or we live by the river or we hold historic rights to withdraw the water for irrigation. When we try and talk about water needs for a state with about thirty-five million people based on deeds and rights that were put in effect better that a century ago, when the population was less than a few million...there just isn't enough water to go around."

"How do you balance it? Limit immigration?"

He gives a strained smile at my lame joke. "Right. That works so well. The problem is that this is now. We have a population that's outstripped both our water resources and our infrastructure and we need to solve it in the present. We can either find ways to move water from the north to Central and Southern California and build more reservoirs, or we can let the Central Valley and parts of the south revert back to semi-arid desert." Hans shakes his head. "Did you know that twenty-five or thirty years ago they put in asparagus farms east of Palm Springs? The Coachella and Imperial valleys are big ag areas now because of irrigation."

How far do I want to research this? I can spend days dredging up old water maps, historic water rights, but in the end it boils down to not enough water, too many demands on it. Something has to give.

We spend another half-hour going over the ins and outs of the details of the tunnel proposals and as I get ready to leave, I'm more confused than ever. One thing is clear, though. Water Resources has to conduct a survey of the underlying land in the Delta to even be able to engineer a route. And this means drilling and pulling up core samples. I ask Hans if he's heard about the dead guy found at the corporation yard.

"I heard about it, yeah. I don't think it has anything to do with the tunnels, or even the survey."

I shake my head. "Maybe not, but there seems to be animosity at the survey. I've heard that some people won't let the survey crews on their land."

"We've had some resistance." Hans acknowledges this with a nod.

"What are you going to do?"

Now he's not happy. "We're going to have to go with eminent domain."

I set my bag down. "Eminent domain" are fighting words with property owners. Add the current anger floating through the Delta like a slough, and it's kerosene to a fire.

"Have you begun?"

"No. A couple of the farmers are talking about suing."

"What would you use eminent domain for? You only want access to an area where you can drill a core sample, you wouldn't be taking much land, would you?" I don't know property law...and don't want to...but I know enough to know that eminent domain transfers the land title to the government.

Hans sighs. "We don't want their land. This has a whole lot of ramifications about ownership of mineral rights, easements, a wheelbarrow full of property law issues. And all we're trying to do is find a way to provide water to the entire state...and the businesses that give us our standard of living."

Before he can begin the litany of the crops that are grown in California, I pick my bag up again, thank him for his time and beat it back to my car. I get to it just as the meter maid makes a turn onto that block. I've beaten a ticket, barely.

I pull out of the parking spot, drive a few blocks to a large discount store and whip into their lot so I can check for messages. Two calls and a text. One call from Phil wanting to ask about some weekend plans he's making, a call from Clarice saying "call me back," and a text, all in caps from her. "WHERE IN HELL ARE YOU?" The call came in twenty-five minutes ago, the text was twenty minutes ago. Apparently she gave up as there's nothing else, so I hit her speed dial number. Now her phone goes to voicemail. I leave her a message to call me and dial Phil's number.

"Hi there, I hope I wasn't interrupting anything." There's a hint of question in his voice.

"No, no. I was in a meeting with the Water Resources PIO and shut my phone off. What are you thinking for the weekend?"

A short silence during which I hear a door shut, then he's back and his voice is warmer. "I was thinking of the San Mateo coast."

"I could do the coast. It'd be nice to get some fresh sea air. Like Half Moon Bay?" I've only been to the small town a few times. When I head to the coast it's usually Santa Cruz and the Monterey Bay beaches.

"I was thinking a bit north, the Moss Beach area. There are some spiffy tide pools at a marine reserve...sea urchins, starfish, anemones. Then we can go for drinks at a place I know."

I don't tell him that almost anything with him is fine by me, but this sounds like a wonderful idea. Some outdoors time, nothing too strenuous for exercise, then drinks at "a place I know." So far, Phil's "places" have been upwards of nine and a half stars on a ten rating.

"That's great! I'll bring some jeans."

"Bring some clothes and shoes you won't mind getting wet. It gets a little splashy. Will I see you Friday night?"

"You will, and I'm looking forward. I'll call you when I leave."

Just as I'm ready to pull out of the lot, my phone lets out the dog song and before I can say anything I hear "Well, thanks for squeezing me into your busy schedule."

"Alright, Clarice, alright. I was in the Department of Water Resources and turned my phone off. What's up?"

There's some crackling, I'm hearing every other word. "Hey, you're breaking up. Let me call you back."

Suddenly she comes through clear. "No need. I'm out in Freeland and it's spotty, but I found a clear place."

"What are you doing in Freeland? Oh, God, don't tell me you're hounding the sheriff's guys about the body? Are the forensics back yet?"

"No, and that's not why I'm here. They found another body." And I completely lose the signal.

CHAPTER EIGHT

Another body. This we can't ignore. I head south and during the thirty-five minute drive to Monroe go over the conversation I want to have with Jim Dodson.

What similarities...weapons, another employee of Earth/Search, time the body was found? What forensics? At least those he'll tell me about.

Did the victims know each other? Have any prior history...maybe working together at a different company? How long had either of them worked at Earth/Search?

I park in the lot behind the *Press* and call Clarice as I head to the Sheriff's office.

"I'm still out here in Freeland," she says as she answers.

"How long will you be? I'm headed over to see if I can catch Sheriff Dodson."

"*You're* going to talk to him?" I feel waves of anger? fear? probably resentment coming through the phone.

"Calm down, Clarice. I just want to have a background talk. I found out today that the state may pull the eminent domain card in order to get the core samples done."

"Ahhh, eminent domain is gonna shake up the foot soldiers out here. You think that could play a part in the murders?"

Did I? "That's pure speculation, a guessing game right now. I assume he's heard about it and I'm curious what plans he has to handle conspiracy theorists."

"You mean...," I can almost hear the gears shift in her head, "that he might expect some kind of stand-off? The Delta farmers against the state drillers?."

"No, nothing that dramatic. But maybe a little civil disobedience. Chaining up the drilling equipment. Demonstrators picketing in front of the trucks. The kind of thing that's a good photo op for the five o'clock news."

"Okayyy." She's not convinced I'm staying out of her turf, but she can't say too much. I am the boss. This is a situation we're aware could edge into an explosion if we're not both careful. I can't step too far and she can't object too much. We've done this dance before.

Jim Dodson *is* in his office and when his admin tells him I'm waiting, he yells, "Come on in Amy."

I'm not always comfortable with his casual greeting. After giving Clarice the stink-eye when she calls him "Jim" I need to keep a professional distance as well. This is a tad hard because he and I have history. He was on a police force in the San Fernando Valley when I was married to my first husband, Vinnie-the-cop.

Vincent Hobbes was killed during a high-speed freeway chase and several hundred police officers turned out for his funeral. Jim Dodson was one of them. I don't remember meeting him but when he was sheriff of neighboring San Juan County we worked on a case together. Now, he's becoming a trusted friend.

"Since you're here by yourself and Clarice is still out in Freeland, I'm guessing you're tag-teaming me on the bodies out there."

"I guess you could call it that," I drop into a visitor's chair in front of his desk and pull out a notebook.

He gives me a sideways glance. "Is this on or off the record?" One eyebrow lifts.

I grin. "Off. Just some background, but my memory is getting unreliable if I don't take *some* notes."

"For you, OK. Just don't tell any of your staff." He smiles back. "What's on your mind."

"I met with the Water Resources PIO today and he mentioned the possibility of eminent domain to get access for the core drilling equipment. The No Delta Tunnels crowd won't take that."

Dodson raises an eyebrow. "Eminent domain? That's not going to be popular. I sure hope they're planning to tell local law enforcement before they move equipment in." He leans back in his chair and his eyes flick to the window. There's not much of a view, mostly the parking lot and then City Hall one street over. I suspect his mind's eye is moving out toward the Delta, taking in the small towns and farms that are liable to become a battleground.

"I don't want to step on Clarice's toes—or yours—but what leads do you have? Do you think these murders have anything to do with the tunnels?"

He groans. "God, Amy, let's bring in a few ancient aliens as well! We haven't notified the next of kin of this guy yet, so there's no telling. I appreciate the tip about what the DWR is up to, but I can't confirm or deny any information about this."

He jumps slightly as his phone rings. "Now my day is complete. There's Clarice. You want to take it?"

I back away so fast he could have been handing me a snake. "Me? Lord no! You have any idea how upset she'd be if I answered your phone!"

"It was just a small joke, Amy," he says as he punches a button and answers. "Sheriff Dodson here."

His half of the conversation is pretty monosyllabic. "No. Not yet. No. Yes. No comment." As he punches off, he looks at me. "I give her about fifteen seconds..." but he's interrupted by the dogs barking from my phone. "Ha, she has you on speed dial." His mouth quirks up in a smile but he's silent as I say, "Hey, Clarice."

"I'm not getting anything out here. These guys are practicing their clam routine. Did you talk to the Sheriff? What did he say."

I back out of Dodson's office and say, "I did. I'm on my way back to the office. Didn't get much. No ID, because no next of kin notification, so no name, no comment on similarities. About the only new thing is that he hadn't heard about the eminent domain possibilities yet."

"He's playing this one close. The only time I got a 'Yes' was when I asked if he was holding a press conference." Her voice is disgusted, but now I know why.

"Did he say when?" I know he didn't, but want to make sure she has something I don't. Not that either of us has enough for more than a tiny brief—"Second body found in Freeland."

As news gathering goes we're still pulling straws, looking for the gold.

"Come on back, Clar. Call him again when you get here, see if he's pulled the press conference together or they found some family to tell. If the guy was local, it could be a short page one."

My little deception in the Sheriff's office bothers me a bit but since my fishing expedition netted me nothing it's only fleeting, doesn't even make it to the guilt level.

Clarice blows into the office a few minutes behind me, waves and heads out again, calling, "Press conference."

In less than half-an-hour she's back.

"That wasn't much. We have his name and a blunt trauma death. But he was an employee of Earth/Search so we have a pattern."

"Alright, Clar. Where was he from?"

She smiles. "The only part that was worthwhile. He lived in Monroe. I'm headed over to find some family or neighbors now. Even shooting for a picture."

True to her instincts, she turns in a good, tight story about Manny Smythe, resident of Monroe, married, three children who moved to Earth/Search from heavy equipment operator because it was "too dangerous" according to the neighbor Clarice rustled up. And bonus points, she's able to borrow a picture of Manny with two of his boys at soccer practice.

There are times when I don't really like my job.

CHAPTER NINE

Why do I think it's a good idea to come to Phil's house on a Friday night?

Traffic is fine until I hit the rise above Vallejo, when all the people wanting to go out in the Bay Area dump onto the freeway. The worst part is even though the freeway gradually expands from two lanes to five lanes, it's still a parking lot and five lanes of stopped traffic makes me realize how many people are cramming into California.

The bridges help space people out with the toll plazas, but I'm cranky as I hunt for parking in and around Russian Hill. I manage to score a spot eight blocks away, thank my little car for fitting and schlep my bag to his building. He's actually lounging on the stoop, watching for me, takes my bag, gives me a one-armed hug and we head up to his apartment.

He drops my bag in his bedroom, comes out and says, "Now, let's do this right," as he sweeps me into a real hug and long, long, long kiss. I feel the tension from the drive slithering down my legs and pooling on the floor and if this keeps up, other things are going to slither down as well.

We pull back and he looks at me, his brown eyes soft with caring.

"I'm so glad you're here. And from the look of you, it was a hellish drive. Want a glass of wine or a drink?"

"Wine, chilled white?" A wine guy, Phil doesn't keep his whites icy cold, but puts a bottle in the refrigerator about thirty minutes before he plans to serve it. Anything more and he says it changes the taste.

Out on his tiny brick patio dug into the hillside I take a deep breath of the cool briny air. It's heaven after the heat in the valley, but I'm learning. I brought a couple of sweaters and a hoodie.

We sit and chat, sharing bits and pieces of our last few days. He tells me about a new exhibition at Yerba Buena Center that's getting reviews in the L.A. papers. I tell him about the bodies in the Delta.

Same career, different focus.

He suggests dinner in one of the Hayes Street Gulch restaurants, behind the Opera House. We take a taxi. Cheaper and easier than trying to drive and park in the city these days.

It's not a late night out. We're both nearing middle age and being quiet together looks better than noisy clubs...plus there are other activities. A nightcap doesn't even sound interesting once we're home and he's kissing me again. He pulls off my sweater, drops his jacket, we shuck off shoes, he pulls my top over my head and looks...for a long moment.

"That's pretty tasty, did you visit Victoria's Secret before you hit the freeway?" A piece of his fine, straight hair falls over an eyebrow, giving him a sexy one-eyed look.

"No, it's just a little something I had around." Not an outright lie, I've had it around for a couple of weeks, sitting in a bag, waiting.

He begins kissing me again, moving his mouth to my earlobe and down my neck as he dances me backward into the bedroom.

Maybe it's because we only see each other a couple of times a month, but when I'm with him, I can't get enough of him. He's a sexy, considerate, experienced lover and we can laugh even as we're making love. I love touching him, holding his hand, stroking his face and when I catch sight of him across a room when we're out together, my breath hitches as I realize he's mine. At least for the night. I don't want to think beyond.

**

The sharp smell of good coffee wakes me. It seems a bit dark and when I pull the curtains aside I see we're wrapped in fog, what the weather forecasts call a "marine layer." It will probably burn off by noon, but it means we have brunch in Phil's kitchen.

Then we're headed south on The Great Highway, passing people with dogs and kids bundled up while beach walking. Phil looks over. "You know it'll clear by the time we're in San Mateo County."

He's right and it does. The parking lot for the Fitzgerald Marine Reserve is starting to fill up and the sun warms the air as we pick our way across the tide pools. I've never spent much time on this kind of beach. The ones I'm familiar with are in Southern California, sandy, smooth and covered with surfers.

There's a primordial feel here, a world in miniature. Small pockets of water hold starfish, sea anemones, snails and tiny fish, all waiting for the tide to sweep in and bring them food. We're careful to keep to the rocks and not step on anything but the swirling water still washes over my feet, soaking my tennies and socks.

I've leaned over so much looking at the tiny universes I think I may have a permanent hunch when Phil says, "Time for a drink."

"Here?" I do a head-turn and take in the ocean, the rocks, the tide pools, a hundred or so people all hunched over looking like gleaners.

"No, there," and he points to a grove of cypress with a white building out on a cliff beyond.

"What's that?"

"That," he says with a grand gesture, "is the Moss Beach Distillery."

At the car, we take time to strip off our wet shoes so when we walk into the restaurant hanging off the cliff we're warmer and comfortable. He steers me through the restaurant to a big terrace at the back and I gasp at the sight of the Pacific, rolling in from Asia. The terrace is furnished with deck chairs and blankets and some of the people seem to have taken up residence.

"This is gorgeous. And it looks old."

Phil smiles. "You like it?"

"Duh! You always have the best surprises. How old is this?"

"Not ancient. It was built in the late 1920s as a speakeasy. Boats anchored and brought their cargos up. It had a big cliental from San Francisco...politicians, movie stars. Dashiell Hammett used to drink here. There's a ghost, too, The Blue Lady."

We have drinks and easy talk as the day wanes and fog begins to drift in, tendrils winding through the cypress forest and hiding the tide pools below us. "Guess no green streak today." Phil's voice sounds rueful. "I thought that would be the perfect end to a perfect day."

I slide my eyes toward him. The green streak. I've never been sure if this is an old wives' tale or a true phenomenon. As the sun dips below the horizon of the Pacific, there's rumored to be a flash of green, maybe some trick of the light or a refraction of the water.

"Have you ever seen one?"

He shakes his head. "No, but I thought this would be an omen for us."

"Hmm..." I stroke my thumb across the back of his hand. There are omens and there are omens, but I don't dare go there.

"I thought maybe it was payback for the Ryde Hotel." On one of his visits to me, I'd taken him on a drive through the Delta to another small restaurant, also a prior speakeasy, where we had drinks and watched the river flow by.

"Not precisely." He leans over to push a piece of wind-blown hair from my face. "That day I realized how much I enjoy your company at out-of-the-way places with a past. I'm glad we have a past. I'm wondering about a future."

I suck in my breath. This I'll have to think about although I can tell my eyes light up when I smile at him.

We walk back to the car with our arms around each other's waist and I rest my hand on this thigh all the way back to his place.

CHAPTER TEN

We make love then lie in bed, drinking coffee and reading bits from the New York *Times* to each other. After hunger drives us out to find brunch we take a taxi to the Ferry Building and wander along the Embarcadero, watching the people out enjoying the sun and water. Gulls dive-bombing kids eating French fries, people whizzing by on skateboards and bikes, tourists with goose-bumped legs taking pictures of one another with the bay as a backdrop.

As the sun drops behind Coit Tower and the air sucks up a chill, we head back. I want to get home before full dark. I'm always loathe to leave him. Not only his presence. But when I'm in the city with him, all my responsibilities strip away and I live for the present.

He carries my bag the eight blocks to my car and tucks it into the passenger's seat.

"I had a great time." We stand with our arms around each other then he lifts a hand and smooths it through my hair. He moves his hand to my face and runs a finger across my lips. "I find that I'm not liking to let you go home."

I close my eyes for a second. "I'm not wanting to go, either. Being with you is..." I'm not sure what the words are so I hug him tighter and reach up to kiss him.

Then I'm in the car, heading for the Bay Bridge and the valley.

What does that last scene with him mean? Are we moving closer, moving too fast? He's saying wonderful words and I may be falling for him. Do I feel more for him than he feels for me? I have a lousy track record with men. I suppose Vinnie couldn't be helped, but when I chose him, I knew he was in a dangerous career. And Brandon....well, my body was engaged but my brain was permanently on vacation when he showed up.

I'd let my body's responses to men lead me down the path to love and betrayal and I swore I'd never do that again. But Phil is different, isn't he? We've known each other and been interested friends for years before we took the dating step. Does this mean I'll be safe with him?

Thinking and second-guessing, I'm on automatic pilot until I come to. I realize I'm in Fairfield and see the sign for Highway 12, the one that winds through the Delta. Reality check. I swing into a gas station and hit Clarice's speed dial.

"Is there a good reason for calling on a Sunday afternoon? A problem?"

Clarice has come over to check on Mac and use the pool. Mac's barking in the background.

"No problems, just wondering how things are. Sounds like you're at my house. I hope you're using the pool."

"It's toasty today and the water feels good. Where are you?"

"I'm in Fairfield, saw a sign for 12 and wondered if anything's popped with the Freeland victims."

Clarice grunts. "Nothing more. I've checked in with the sheriff's office every day but they say nothing new."

"Have you checked calls for domestics out there?"

It's quiet on her end, then, "Amy, you asked me to do that then headed for the city. Yesterday was Saturday and today's Sunday. I'll give you that I love researching, but I also like some time off. I have it as first to do tomorrow."

Mental head-slap. I've verbalized my stream-of-consciousness and dumped it on her.

"Sorry, Clar...my mind's just running off at the mouth. Want to grab a quick dinner? I'm about an hour out."

"Yeah, OK. Not too late, though. I have a lot for tomorrow."

Now Phil's flown and I'm focused on Clarice. I'd always been wary of forming a to-close friendship with her. I'm her boss and I thought I'd kept the lines clear. Lately I've felt them wavering and Clarice has come within kissing distance of insubordination.

I'm going to have to have a come-to-Jesus meeting with her and find another dog-sitter and now I've pushed her buttons. "See you in a bit, then."

I wheel back on the freeway kicking myself. Going into the pleasure zone about Phil puts my brain into some idle space where things miss filters on the way out of my mouth. I need to get those filters up and running before Clarice and I have a sit-down.

The air has been on in my car and it's a jolt when I step out in my driveway. Clarice's right, it's toasty and then some. She and Mac are out in back and he comes tearing up to say hello, making me do a little step so I don't get knocked down.

"Hi, hi, hi..." I scrub his ears and lean over to give him a hug. He's a mixed breed with Scottie predominant but somebody in his background was big. He weighs about sixty-five pounds, is built like a tank but is a big sissy.

Clarice and I head for a downtown diner and both order salads. It's too hot to chew on much else.

"So, di1d you have a good time with Phil?" She's working off her miff by stuffing baby greens in.

"I did." I give her an abbreviated rundown, then say, "Have you seen Jim?"

She begins to choke, takes a sip of water, sputters. "You mean Sheriff Dodson?"

"Alright, this is off the clock and away from the office."

"We went out to dinner and a movie in Sacramento last night." She's so fair she can't hide the sudden flash of red fleeting over her face.

"You're staying away from current cases?" This is always a big pitfall with journalists being involved with sources, particularly law enforcement. There are huge gaps of silence and tip-toeing around landmines, even in innocent conversations.

Clarice is stabbing a beet and I know it's my heart she's after. "Yes, Amy. If you don't think I'm professional, I'd think you think Jim is."

Here's the opening and I pick my words like she's picking through her salad. "I do think you're a professional, Clarice, but I'm afraid I've let the lines blur a bit. I haven't wanted to pull rank, but I'm feeling like you're overstepping boundaries and I've let you."

"What? You're the one who pushes me, you're the one who gives me those goofy assignments..."

"Stop right there, Clarice. That's the attitude I'm talking about. I feel like you're taking some of my actions as weaknesses. A little back-and-forth is fine but arguments and snide remarks are taking over. I'm sorry if I've taken advantage of you to watch Mac. I'll make other arrangements next time."

Now the red tide pulls out. She's pale, her pupils are dilated and her mouth gapes. She's making sounds, trying to form words. "Oh, no, Amy...uh...I didn't think...I'm sorry. I thought I was just being funny, flip. I didn't mean to be snide. I admire you. You're the mentor I never had in school. And I want you as a friend. I know it looks like I'm tired of being told to watch dating a cop, but I appreciate your advice. I know you've been there and know how hard it is.

"Even though I moan and groan at some of the assignments, I trust your news judgment. I do know there are other interesting things besides the cops and crime."

Her eyes are shining with wetness. Who knew Clarice had such a soft center? I need to keep the lines clear, and call her when she nears the insubordination line, but I don't want her to lose her edge and enthusiasm.

"Is this going in my file? Are you writing me up?"

"No, this is a warning. We both need to pull back and watch the boundaries. I do need to ask again about your conversations with Jim. It's hard not to talk about current events. With Phil, we understand the quirks and pressures of the media, but we have such different interests."

"I'm fine with Jim, Amy. I don't know where we'll end up but I enjoy being around him. Mostly I pump him for his past in L.A. It gives me a better idea of how cops work and he likes to talk about old cases." She's subdued as she sets her fork and napkin down, and the red tide of pique? embarrassment? is gone.

I let the talk drift off as we both check phones for the time or messages. We head off in different directions and I'm home before ten, in time to be ready for bed with a book when Phil calls.

"I see you're home. Was it a bad drive?" His words are matter-of-fact, but his tone has underlying messages.

"Not too bad. A little traffic. It's easier when I'm going the wrong way. Clarice watched Mac so we went out for dinner. We had words. I'm upset. I can talk to you later about it. I'm in bed with a book, now."

"A book? That's a competition I can handle." He gives a soft laugh and glosses over Clarice.

The comment and his voice bring memories from this morning washing over me. After we say good-night, I turn off my light and lay in the warm dark, replaying.

CHAPTER ELEVEN

Conspiracies run through my dreams. I know today I have to put my friend Nancy, the reference librarian, at the top of the agenda.

We met a few years ago when our daughters were friends in school. Now hers, Becky, is married with two kids. She chose a different road than Heather and the girls have drifted apart—Nancy and I are still together.

I have a surface understanding about eminent domain and wonder what about it gives some people the willies. Sure, it takes away some private property rights. The state going in and riding rough-shod over individuals, though? I never understood Ruby Ridge and Waco and those guys who drive around in pick-ups with bumper-stickers about being afraid of the government.

Probably I should do some research on the Posse Comitatus while I'm at it.

Nancy's on the phone, waves me in to the reference section and holds up a "wait" finger. As she comes over she's shaking her head.

"What can I do for you? At least I know you won't ask me to do your kid's senior project." We've both been asked to do things beyond our scope. She gets requests to search for primary source material for student papers and I get an overzealous teacher who grades his kids on whose letter to the editor gets printed. Great way to teach and instill the value of doing your own work.

"Talk to me about Posse Comitatus," I say and watch her eyes widen.

She takes a couple of breaths. "Why are you looking at those crazies? They're dangerous and scary."

"I know that much about them, right-wing haters who want to obliterate all forms of central government. Do we have any around here?"

"Hmmm...I don't think so" She's walking back into the stacks talking over her shoulder and I'm trailing along feeling like a yappy little dog.

She stops so fast I run into her. "Wait a minute." She taps her finger on her lips. "Kathy, no not Kathy...Karen. Yeah, Karen...hang on." Her eyes light up. "Karen Mathews!" She's looking as though she won the lottery.

"Alright, I give. Who's Karen Mathews?"

"Probably before your time. She was the clerk-recorder for Stanislaus County for about ten years. Refused to remove an IRS lien against one of the anti-tax people and got some threats. Let's see..." She digs through some microfiche, slides it around on the viewer. "Aha." She's found a story.

"The IRS slapped a $416,000 property lien and she refused to remove it. In 1994 a guy ambushed her in her garage, kicked her, stabbed her, sexually assaulted her and put a gun to her head. He pulled the trigger three times but no bullets."

"My God! Was he part of the Posse?"

"It doesn't say. He was from Oregon, served time in federal prison. Let's see what else we have." She moves to a computer, begins a search. "Bingo. He served eighteen years and was released to a half-way house in the San Joaquin Valley."

She sits back and we look at each other. It's a tenuous thread but if we follow it into the deep woods of conspiracy, it may yield some links.

I need to sit down with this information and Clarice. Regardless of our discussion, she's still the best researcher and reporter I have. And this is in her bailiwick. If she's going to poke around in the past, I want her to do it quietly. He's proved dangerous in the past. We have no reason to think he's going to hook up with any of the folks in the Delta...nor do we have any concrete information that there's a group formed to fight eminent domain.

It bears watching, but right now it's partially-formed tidbits floating around in a caffeine overdose.

I make notes for Clarice. I'll send her over later this afternoon to dig around more and then have her run any names.

Nancy and I head out for a quick lunch and catch up with girl gossip. I tell her I'm planning a graduation party later this summer for Heather. "I'm so pleased for her. It's been a long road—for both of us."

"Why later? Doesn't she graduate in a couple of weeks?"

I nod. "Yeah, but she's cutting it close. She's coming up this weekend to find a place then she's moving right after graduation and starts with her preceptor in three days."

"That's fast!"

"I think she's relieved to get school over with and get to her real life. She's matured a lot in this last year. Do you think Becky would help get the gang together? I've lost track of who's still around."

Nancy's fishing through her wallet to pay the bill and looks up. "I'm sure she'd help. She doesn't see a lot of the kids now that she's a young mom." There's silence, then, "God, remember when we met through our kids? It seems like yesterday."

I start to say, "It was," then realize Nancy's a grandmother. The world has changed. My grandmother was *old!* Probably not, but I wonder what Nancy's grandkids think when they look at her...a vibrant woman holding down a responsible job, respected in the community, not home baking cookies.

We catch each other's eye and crack up, knowing that we're both wondering where time went.

I walk with her back to the library. "I don't have anything scheduled this afternoon, so send Clarice over any time."

Clarice. Hmmm... "I wanted to talk about Clarice. I had to speak with her last night."

"Uh, oh, that doesn't sound good." She waves me into her tiny office, moves a pile of books to the floor and says, "Sit. Talk."

I give her the abbreviated version.

"I've notice she's getting a little too comfortable around you." Nancy's trying to stack the papers on her desk into some semblance of neatness. "Do you think this talk will help?"

"I think so. She looked as though she was on the verge of tears. Apologized...lord, I feel so crummy about it. I'm mad at myself for letting it get to this point and mad at her for pushing it to this point. I should have said something earlier."

"It's good that you finally addressed it. I know Clarice is one of the best you have. Not many people talk about the paper, but I've heard quite a few compliments on her stories. And you two are developing a friendship outside of work. I think she's going to be in touch with you for most of her career because of the path you've set her on."

"I hope so. There are some journalists who seem to be born for the job. Clarice is one of those. She has such energy. She loves tracking down esoteric pieces of information. She's not afraid of the grunt work and she lives to ask bad guys why they did it. With all of her brusqueness, she's wonderful at getting victims and their families to talk about the pain. She did that amazing story on the hooker who was killed in the vineyard last fall." That story was so good I insisted she enter it in contests. We're still waiting to hear from a couple, including the Pulitzer, but I don't hold much hope for that.

I stand up, knocking over a stack of books. "Sorry, maybe this has gotten to me. Thanks for listening. I mentioned it to Phil last night but didn't go into it."

"Phil's for another lunch." Nancy laughs. "And we may need some wine. Glad to listen and I don't think you and Clarice are broken. Maybe bent, but fixable. Send her over."

"Will do," I say over my shoulder as I head back to the *Press*.

CHAPTER TWELVE

I've left a "come talk to me" note on Clarice's screen. I'm engrossed in reading copy when she taps at my door.

"You wanted to see me?"

She's taken the talk to heart and although I needed to do it, it's bittersweet to see the new Clarice. The talk must have shaken her, she's not just bursting in.

"I did." I wave at a chair in front of my desk. "This may take a bit."

She pales. Does she think I'm disciplining her? I thought I was clear last night.

"I've been over at the library talking with Nancy about the Posse Comitatus."

She frowns. I've stumped her. "The who...or what?"

"The Posse Comitatus. It's a loose knit group of right-wing fanatics who believe that there shouldn't be any government higher than the county level and that state and federal governments don't have the right to tax citizens. They were active a few years ago, but I'm not sure they're still around."

"What do they have to do with us? Is there some threat I missed?"

"No, not yet. But the issue of eminent domain is one the Posse could take on as a conspiracy cause."

Clarice jots a few words in her notebook, looks up. "Do you want a story?"

"No, this is just background in case something busts loose. Nancy will fill you in on some sources. These guys are really scary—check out Karen Mathews—and I want you to know about them."

"I have some time. I checked with the cops and the sheriff's departments and nothing new on either of the murders. Probably all I have is a cops log brief for tonight."

Every night Clarice, or a fill-in reporter, goes to the police and sheriff's departments and notes a few of the more interesting calls they've gotten that day. Some days it's only a disturbance or brandishing a weapon or a parole violation, but this way the neighborhoods know why the cops and sirens showed up. And the police see it as a positive that we're recording them at work, earning the taxpayers' money.

"That's fine. Have you had a chance to check the domestic disturbance calls in the Delta yet?"

She shakes her head, knocking loose a piece of hair that falls into her eye. "I'm doing that tomorrow. The records clerk who usually helps me is out today." She turns to head out, then shoots back over her shoulder, "It's probably a waste of a fishing expedition." I can see a cheeky grin reflected in my office window. It's good to know that I haven't squashed her spirit.

Soon, I'm going to have to buckle down and write that damn editorial about the tunnel proposition. I go online to research and read everything I can find pro and con. I'm not sure how I feel. On the surface, it's a good idea to equalize the water available to every Californian, but until the huge oil boom in the early twentieth century, not very many people chose to live in the dry, dusty Los Angeles basin. Once it was planted with houses and people, the Department of Water and Power sucked the water from the Owens Valley of the Eastern slope of the Sierra, among other projects.

Southern California wasn't the only place that went after water. The East Bay Municipal Utilities District put dams on the Mokelumne to feed growing Alameda County and San Francisco dammed up and filled Hetch Hetchy valley as its reservoir for water. Hetch Hetchy was a high Sierra glacial valley that John Muir called more beautiful than Yosemite.

There's no easy or right answer for water in California and the drought years exacerbate the problems. During one serious drought, some small towns in the Central Valley ran out of water pulled from wells because the aquifer had been so depleted.

I'm going to keep reading until the election is so close that I *have* to make a choice. In the meantime, I'll let this stay fallow.

There's talk again of instituting year-round school to ease the crowded facilities and Sally is headed to what may be a raucous school board meeting tonight. We spend half an hour framing story ideas for a couple of different scenarios and I'm thankful again that Heather got through school relatively unscathed by these facility issues.

Things are quiet, so I go home for an early night, remembering that last time I did this some loons took over a convenience store, kept three people hostage and held up our deadline until after eleven at night. Luckily, the cops managed to resolve it with no injuries—well, a little tear gas damage—and we still made the morning edition.

Mac is overjoyed to see me, although I don't think he can tell time. I'm not even sure he remembers that I was gone for two days but he's been stuck to me since I got back.

It's still too hot for a walk so he paces beside the pool while I ease through some laps and we have a brief toss the ball game. I flip on the local news—a treat to watch in my kitchen, I'm usually at my desk at this time—while I fix our dinner. Dog food for him, a Greek salad for me. Gone are the days when I actually cooked a meal and Brandon, Heather and I sat down to eat as a family. Don't miss him, do miss her, and I'll have to shop for groceries before she shows up Friday night.

After it cools, after a walk, I call Heather to get an ETA and ask if she's made any other plans. I'm wise to her homecomings now, since a couple of times I'd planned a fancy meal only to have her call and say she was out with friends and not to wait up.

She sends off some pheromones or ESP waves or something every time she comes home. Less than an hour after she hits the front door, the phone calls to her start. It's uncanny and a phenomenom that the communication industry needs to investigate.

CHAPTER THIRTEEN

Thoughts of Clarice spin in my head most of the night. Is she headed into danger from the tunnel protesters? Are there members of right wing conspiracy groups active in the Delta? I'm not rested and finally give up trying to sleep when the sun hits my bedroom window. I stagger to the kitchen and make coffee while Mac charges out to the back to do his business and let the squirrels know the big guy is here.

Since I'm up earlier than usual, I take Mac for a walk in the relative morning cool. We start down a different block this morning and I hear a machine, a backhoe or bulldozer, and loud ripping sounds. Around a corner, I see cyclone fencing encircling a house and a backhoe tearing chunks of the building apart and throwing them into a huge dumpster.

There's too much noise to talk to any of the workers so I mumble the name of the construction company a dozen times, hoping I'll remember it until I get home. It shouldn't be too hard, it's ABC Construction.

I find their website, send the link to my work email and plan to check it out later. Not many houses are demolished in my slightly upscale neighborhood. Is the owner looking to build one of those lot-line-to-lot line McMansions? How did he get it through the zoning and building departments? A small mystery to begin the day.

A skim through the *Press* and two of the metro dailies, a bagel, a handful of food and fresh water for Mac, a shower, ten minutes of staring in my closet and I'm ready to go. A sleeveless summer dress, a lightweight cotton sweater tied around my shoulders, a pair of sandals and minimum make-up. No sense in spending a lot of time on it, if I go out in the heat today, it'll just melt off my face.

It's quiet when I walk into the newsroom and I send a memo to all to make sure they let me know what's coming in. Then I hit the ABC Construction site and plug the neighbor's address in their "current projects" listing. Odd, nothing comes up.

On to the Monroe building department's site and there's a demolition permit for the address with an asterisk. Paging down, I find that the permit was issued to the California Department of Justice.

What?

The DOJ site requires searching for "demolition" until it gives up the information that certain properties can be taken by eminent domain and demolished if drugs were manufactured on the premises.

OMG, a drug lab in my neighborhood? Why didn't I know this?

I'm beginning to steam, then take a deep breath. If this was a drug house, they're tearing it down now. For some reason, they weren't public about this. This is the kind of digging that Clarice loves and excels at. A flagged email AND a red "See me" note will get a quick response when she comes in.

In the meantime, I call Jim Dodson. The demolished house isn't in his jurisdiction, but he can give me some background on the eminent domain used by law enforcement. And I want to chat conspiracy theories with him.

"Hi Amy." His voice is calm this morning, telling me he can take some time to talk. "I'm tied up in meetings this afternoon, but free this morning. Can you come over now?"

I'm reaching for my purse as I say, "I'll be there in a few minutes. Thanks, Sheriff."

It's already starting to warm. Running errands before noon is a given in summer in the valley. Not for the first time, I regret that we've never gone to the European model of naps in the afternoon.

The air is running at the Sheriff's office. Is this harder on the deputies if they suddenly have to go out in the heat? What about the SWAT guys? Or the bomb team? Putting on all that gear and moving around when it's 106 degrees has to be a killer. My brain segues to the firefighters, too, and I get a rush of caring for all these people.

Jim is in the break room, drinking coffee and chatting with one of the lieutenants. He offers me a cup and we head back to his office.

"What's up?" he says as he swivels into his chair. "I don't see you as much as Clarice any more."

Is this a statement that she's here too much? I can't delve into second or third guesses at hidden messages in his conversations. I'm beginning to learn that men most often mean just what they say.

"I've been busy trying to figure out this Delta tunnel thing. Is it good or bad? Is it good for farmers and Southern California and bad for the Delta? Will it restore wetlands? Lord, I wish I had a crystal ball, or a peek at twenty-five years in the future." I move a coaster with an FBI seal over and set my coffee down.

"I know." Dodson pushes a stack of papers aside and leans his elbows on the desk. "I've lived, well, we've both lived, in Southern California and know how precious water is. I have no idea if this plan is a solution or a panacea for agribusiness."

He huffs. "One thing for sure is that the Delta folks are up in arms about it."

"I want to talk about that. We've heard some grumblings over eminent domain. Does law enforcement use it? And do you have to forcibly move people out and seize property?"

"Hah! It looks like you're imagining those nineteenth century English engravings...the starving widow and her kids tossed out in the street. Sometimes we provide security, but even with eminent domain the property owner gets payment."

"I'm curious about the possibility of eminent domain in the Delta. That's not buying property, just the rights to drilling core samples. How does that work?"

Dodson grimaces. "I'm not sure. The lawyers are going to have to sort that out. If the Delta people file suit, that'll drag through court for a few years. With luck, I'll be gone."

My mouth hangs open. Is he telling me he's moving? Looking for another job? Has he been recruited somewhere else? I need to ask Clarice if she's heard anything.

"Whether or not they file a suit, have you heard any conspiracy theories?"

"Oh, sure. 'They're going to breach some levees and flood our land.' 'They're going to divert the entire Sacramento River and send the water south.' 'We're gonna join the state of Jefferson and secede from California.'."

That last one isn't new. In 1941 four southern Oregon and three northern California counties banded together and declared themselves the State of Jefferson, complaining that neither state paid much attention to the sparsely populated areas. It wasn't lost on a lot of people that this area was also the Klamath River Basin and comprised a huge federal land swath under the Bureau of Land Management. The idea of Jefferson has come back now and its supporters claim an additional four California counties will sign on.

There's also a petition by a Silicon Valley capitalist, Tim Draper, to cut California into six separate states. It doesn't look like this will gain enough signatures to make it on the ballot in 2016.

So much for the California ideal of celebrating our diversity. Some folks only want to hang around with like-minded pals. How much of this secessionist talk is enough to be dangerous?

CHAPTER FOURTEEN

I watch dust motes swirl around in the shaft of morning sun. Dodson and I are quiet for a few heartbeats trying to grasp what anger or disappointment could cause this reaction. We look at each other and say, "Ruby Ridge..." simultaneously.

"Do you think there's enough resentment out there for something like that?" I can't imagine tensions escalating to that level.

Dodson shakes his head. "I don't know. It's pretty foreign to me."

"What about the Posse Comitatus?"

His head jerks up. I've startled him. "Have you heard that any of them are involved?" His question could be accusatory.

"No, no. I was just doing some research at the library and the Karen Mathews case came up."

"I wasn't here, but of course I heard about that case." He's pensive, casting his mind back. "Was he a Posse member?"

"I don't think so, but he believed the IRS had no right to put a lien on his property. And Mathews filed it anyway. Are there any members here?"

"I have no idea. They're pretty loosely organized. None of my guys have seen flyers announcing a meeting at the local rec center." We both snort.

"I'm probably just borrowing trouble." I drain my cup. "I've asked Clarice to research them, but I'm nervous. That's a hornets' nest I want her to take care with. Have you gotten the autopsy reports back yet?"

From his expression, I realize my change of topic has started down a track that left Dodson on a siding. "Oops, sorry. Sometimes I just wander around in my own head then open my mouth. The autopsies on the two guys from the corporation yard in Freeland."

"Whoa, Amy, I've watched Clarice do that, but never you. Did you guys learn it from each other?" He smiles and his eyes crinkle. I'm glad he can appreciate our oddities.

"Most of the time we're creating stories. Either wading through what we want to ask, and wondering why this is important, or wrestling with how we want to write it...tell the story with the most impact. It makes for a solitary life when you're working. Of course, everyone always knows what I'm thinking...hah." I shake my head. More often than not I think everyone hears the conversations in my head.

"I've had to learn to work through what I want to say before I start to speak. There are some things I just can't talk about. That's a lesson I learned from folks like you." He smiles again, taking some of the sting out of his words.

Law enforcement can be very wary around the press, accusing us of misquoting them, of reporting things wrong, of sensationalizing stories to gain attention. Some journalists fall into those categories and some media...tabloids and slanted broadcasts... will go for the blood every time. A lot of us, though, are proud of what we do and how we do it and are careful to get it right.

"Well?"

"Ah, the autopsies. It's probably no surprise but both of the workers were killed by blunt force trauma to the head."

"And the weapons?"

"The medical examiner says, 'Consistent with a round, heavy piece of equipment or pipe, probably metal.' That leaves pretty much everything that's not tied down at the yard. We're looking at some tools for any blood or hair, but it's almost impossible. And even if we find the actual weapon, this may be a crime of opportunity. What's the motive, besides anger?"

Dodson glances at me, suddenly aware that he's said a lot more than he intended to. I nod and pick up my purse, showing him that I haven't taken any notes during our conversation. A sign that this is all off the record.

Since he's been so open, I feel guilty about what I overheard at the nail salon. I clear my throat and say, "I heard a funny thing last week. There were two women getting their nails done, and one of them said that Suzy's husband will probably beat her up for allowing the surveyor into their back yard."

"Sounds like a domestic violence incident. What does this have to do with our bodies?"

"The two women talking were neighbors of Suzy's...and they all live in the Delta, in a spot that's targeted for drilling."

He's making notes on a small pad, then taps his finger on his lips. "Neither of the victims were surveyors. They drove the trucks for the equipment, but didn't operate any of the drills. They just seem to be random victims."

"Maybe random, but the only reason they were in Freeland was because of the core sample drilling and the tunnels. Would they have been killed if they were at some other job site?"

"Damn, Amy, want to come to work with me? That's just the problem, we don't know. Was there something in the prior or personal lives of these two guys that marked them for death? Or was it the location and the job that made them vulnerable? I have officers out at both ends, but can't find any links yet. Even have the Highway Patrol working this."

My eyes round. "The Highway Patrol?" Highway patrol officers are also the state police. Even though they're much better known for their highway duties—thanks CHiPs—they're all sworn officers and work investigations.

"Freeland is in my jurisdiction, but the corporate yard was built for a state project. It's only drilling now, a contract with the state to provide core samples. I'm sure the company will have to work closely with the state on drawing the map for the tunnel construction. If people are getting killed over the idea of the tunnels, for sure the state has an interest."

I realize he's right. If there're organized forces trying to stop the tunnels, who are they? How far will they go? Even scarier and harder to track, are there individuals working alone?

"This is making me concerned for Clarice."

"Clarice? I thought you said she was just doing research."

"She is. Now. You know Clarice, though. If she finds interesting stuff, she's going to follow it up. She'd likely follow it to a Posse, or some other conspiracy, meeting. If they have meetings."

Dodson is quiet, weighing his personal responses against any law enforcement needs. "Do you have any suggestions? Can you pull her off the story if it gets dangerous?"

Good thing I'd finished my coffee or it would be all over his desk. "Pull her off? You're kidding. Clarice is a pit bull with a story like this. The best we can do is give her an escort, or watcher. Someone who's available to get her out of a bad situation."

"I don't have the staff to put a guard on her. I can assign one deputy to keep a loose tail on her. Maybe just when she's out in the Delta?"

"That should be enough. I may be overreacting and I don't think she's in any danger now. Please don't ever let her know we had this conversation. She'd be royally pissed, and I couldn't blame her. These conspiracy guys, if that's who we're up against, really frighten me. Maybe when she's read the Mathews files, she'll get an idea of the lengths they'll go to."

I stood and had a flash of nausea. Was I trying to keep Clarice safe, or trying to clip her wings, keeping her from the job she loved...plus interfering in her personal life with a man she was interest in?

I never did well on tightropes.

CHAPTER FIFTEEN

"What a story! I'd love to come across this." Clarice is flushed as she rounds the door into my office. From the heat?

"Which story?"

"The Mathews one, that weird guy. The Posse Comitatus."

Not flushed from the heat, flushed from the chase. I don't think my sending her on a research mission has been a cautionary tale.

"Didn't it make you a little nervous? How much more did you find about the Posse?"

She fans her notebook, stoops to pick up a fallen pen, brushes her hair off her forehead, manages to put a stripe of ink into her hairline, says "Not a lot around here. They're so loosely organized they almost work independently," and flops down in a chair.

It seems that my fears of curbing her are unfounded...she's back.

"I wanted you to be aware of them in case you heard something."

She nails me with a look. "Do you think there are any of them in the Delta? Surely no farmers would go to those extremes to keep the surveyors and drillers away."

"Probably not. Most of the Posse members live in sparsely populated areas, places like Idaho and Montana, not the Delta. We may think the conspiracy theorists are only the looney right fringe, but they can be dangerous. Have you talked with the clerk about domestic calls yet?"

Clarice nods and I can almost see her biting her tongue to hold back a snarky comment. "I talked to her before I headed to the library. She said she'd do a search and call me if she found anything." Her cell rings as she's talking to me, she says, "Yep, yep...really? I'm on my way," to the caller and collects her stuff.

"She found three calls to the same address in the last six months. Somebody at that house has been busy, or angry. I'll check the logs for briefs while I'm there," and waves as she sails out the door.

I'm glad I had that conversation with Jim Dodson. Far from frightening Clarice off, the scent of a story with implications of conspiracy or danger whets her appetite.

Rats. She's run out before I have a chance to have her check the demolition permit. I text her to call me and pull up "California water" on LexisNexis and Google. This will keep me occupied for the rest of the day.

I'm clicking through droughts and floods over the years and stumble across The Great Flood of 1862. In December 1861 and January 1862 a weather pattern formed over the West Coast and it rained so much that floods washed out farms and settlements from the Columbia River south to San Diego and as far east as what's now the states of Idaho and Nevada.

The flooding was so extensive that it bankrupted the state of California, dependent on property taxes. The governor, state legislature and state employees weren't paid for more than a year and the state's economy shifted from farming to ranching.

I was looking for drought and found water...way, *way* too much water. It's feeling as though I'm channeling Goldilocks; too much, too little, but nothing just right. Clearly something had to be done, so the levees and some of the state water projects were created. Is it time for another massive state program to distribute water, now in the *way* too little category?

My eyes are crossing from reading on the computer when Clarice taps the door frame, bustles in and sits. She notices it takes a second for me to focus on her and a wisp of annoyance adds a frown line. As suddenly as it appears, it's gone and I give her a star for keeping it to herself.

"What do you want first?" Like a cat with prey, she teases me, relishing her news.

"Hmmm, the domestics?"

"Your ladies were right, Suzy has an abusive husband. All the domestic calls in the Delta during the last six months were to her house. The cops separated them, took him to jail to cool off and released him. The last time, he actually got before a judge and was sentenced to two months of anger management classes. They don't seem to have helped."

I put my head in my hands. This isn't news that helps anyone. It's a revolving door in the justice system. The women don't want to report it... because it's shameful, because the next time it'll escalate, because he swears he'll never do it again, because she loves him and he loves her. And most times the guys get off scot-free, do it again, it escalates and she may end up dead.

"Think it's time to hit the Delta again?" I'm wracking my brain to find a hook for this story. Clarice showing up and asking Suzy about the relationship with her husband isn't going to get her past the screen door.

Clarice is game, though. "I can knock on a few neighbor's doors so it doesn't look like I'm targeting her. Ask her how she feels about the core drilling and the tunnel proposal. She may start talking."

"If her husband is home, ask some softball questions on the tunnels." I have a mild frisson of fear, sending Clarice out to a house of violence.

I see the beginnings of a glower before she catches herself. She settles for, "Jeez, Amy, I'm a big girl. Thanks for being concerned, though."

"Wait a minute. I keep forgetting to ask you." I run through with her what I've learned about demolition permits filed by the DOJ. "I'm thinking it must have been a drug house, but why weren't we notified?"

She shrugs as she heads out the door. "Don't know. I'll follow up on it tomorrow. They probably didn't think it was worthwhile telling us. If they've gotten to demolition, any bust must have happened months or even years ago. Maybe they figure no one remembered."

She may be right but I'd still like to know. I plug the address into our own morgue files, but no hits come up, which means whatever caused the DOJ to get involved, we didn't know about it. Next, I go to the county's assessor's files. What comes up is the name of the last owner to pay taxes on the parcel. It's a man at an Arizona address, but the taxes have been in arrears for almost seven years.

Odd. Why didn't the property get put up for sale for back taxes? They still hold those sales on the steps of the county courthouse, a throwback to the days when "public" didn't mean mass or social media.

There's enough on my desk, and my mind, that I need to start a clean-up and to-do list. I scan the piles and debate using the topple filing system—anything that falls on the floor gets tossed—then sigh and begin picking through and reading. Yeah, yeah, I read the minute manager and the guru who said only handle a piece of paper once, but I'm a sucker for odd, weird bits of information.

I do have a file for future projects, though it's an elastic definition. Some may not turn out to even be worth a story. Just things I've heard or read somewhere. By the time I get to the note about orange paint on the freeway...a note I've looked at at least half-a-dozen times...I've killed the better part of an hour and filled my wastepaper recycling basket.

This time, I write a note to Gwen to check out the paint and toss the note. I've handled this piece of paper *way* too many times.

The stories for tomorrow's paper from the reporters are waiting to be read, and I still need to make a list and hit the grocery store. Heather will be home in a couple of days and I'd better be prepared for large young men hanging around my pool and refrigerator.

CHAPTER SIXTEEN

Phil calls as I get home and we talk for a longish time. I tell him my qualms about possibly exposing Clarice to danger and he pooh-poohs them.

"Those fringe people always get a lot more press than they're worth, you know that. I've never heard any mention of the Posse here. They're not interested in urban areas where there's a lot of law enforcement and government involvement."

"You're probably right." Talking to Phil helps to anchor some of my free-floating anxieties. "There have been two killings out there, though. And the Sheriff is at a loss so far."

"Dodson seems like a pretty sensible guy, Amy. Have you talked to him?"

Jim Dodson and Phil have met on a few occasions and Phil and I have had dinner with Clarice and the Sheriff. Acquaintances, not friends.

I do a recap of my conversation with Dodson and the fact that he's willing to keep a loose watch in the Delta. "He's concerned that he doesn't have any leads yet. So far, the only thing that links the two victims is that they both worked for the same company and were found at the same place."

"There's a link, you and he just haven't found it."

"I know. I get impatient. Guess I read too many murder mysteries where everything falls into place."

There's a soft laugh. One of the things I appreciate about Phil is his willingness to react to my lame jokes and bad puns. An off-beat sense of humor is gold in a relationship and I rank it above how a guy looks in a tuxedo—highly sexy.

Phil makes a sound in his throat and his voice deepens. "One of the things I like about you is the way your mind works. You can link outrageous bits together and it makes sense. It gives me some bread crumbs to follow."

"Bread crumbs?" I'm tingly at the tone of his voice, but don't understand.

"It shows me a path to getting to know you better. I'm following it and I like where it's leading. A lot."

Silence. From both of us. Then, "I miss you. Spending time with you takes a load of worries off. I find that I'm in the present when we're together. Like in *Brave New World*, 'I take a gram and only am.' "

Now he snickers. "You're quoting Huxley to me? See, that's what I'm talking about. I'm not sure I want to be compared to a mood-altering drug though."

"I mean it in the best possible way. I spend too much time trying to change the past and manipulate the future that I forget to enjoy the now."

His bantering, sexy tone is gone. "You're trying to change the past? That's not a sign of good mental health."

"Not changing it, I guess. I spend too much time on the 'what ifs'. What if Vinnie hadn't been killed? What if I hadn't married Brandon? What if I hadn't dragged Heather out of her comfort zone and half-way across the state? I keep hoping that the past can help me make decisions in the future."

"And have you found it helps?"

"Of course not. I just can't stop it. That's why I love being with you." Ooops, I said the "L" word. I hold my breath.

The dark tones are back in his voice as he says, "And I love spending time with you. Weekend after next is ours."

We have a few more minutes talking about Monterey. He says he has some restaurants in mind and will "surprise" me with the accommodations.

After we hang up his voice is still in my ear, conjuring images of a room steps from the waves with the bark of seals and the screaming of gulls the only accompaniments to the night. I shiver. This is my immediate future and it's coming none too soon.

It's been a warming conversation, but what does it mean? Am I getting in too deep? Reading emotions into our talk that Phil may not feel? I've always warned Heather against falling in love with love, instead of the person. Am I doing that? Trying to recreate the impulses I felt at the beginning with Brandon and ignoring the subtle signs that he wasn't what he portrayed?

No. Phil and I have known each other too long. Been through several partners each. Have three marriages between us. I want to take this slowly. I care for him deeply. Do I love him? I don't know yet.

Later, thoughts of Phil override any worries about Clarice and I come awake in the morning with a small bubble of happiness in my chest. This lasts until my phone rings as I'm about to head for work.

"What's up, besides you so early?" Clarice doesn't come in to work until noon and stays in bed as long as she can.

"I just got a call. Suzy's in the hospital in bad shape."

"What happened?" That's a dumb question where Suzy's concerned.

Clarice sounds as though she's talking to a mildly deficient child. "Her husband beat her up. Again."

Deep breath. I asked for that. "I mean, what are the injuries? Did he shoot her or anything?"

"I don't know. I just got off the phone. I'm not ready to go yet. I thought you might want to swing by the hospital on your way and get more details."

Clarice is giving away a possible source and story? "I can do that. Have you called the sheriff's office yet?"

"No, I only called you. I'm planning on going into the sheriff's office this morning rather than calling. It might be harder to ignore me in person. I'll check in as soon as I'm through."

The hospital is less than a mile from my house. Five minutes after I hang up with Clarice, I'm in the ER, asking about Suzy. I flash my press credentials, but all I can get out of the gatekeeper is that she's been admitted and is "resting comfortably."

We have confirmation that something's happened, but more information will have to wait until Clarice gets in from talking to Dodson...or more likely one of the deputies. My office is too small to pace, plus I have several reporters giving me the fish eye, so I call them in to ask about their stories coming today.

Not anything exciting, but Gwen has tracked down the truck hauling orange paint and is working it into a nice, short feature.

The reason that the orange paint looks so familiar is that it's paint for the Golden Gate Bridge, a special formula. Somewhere on its journey along the California freeways from the paint factory to the south and the bridge to the north, a drum tipped over and leaked. Not the whole fifty-five gallons, just enough to drip out under the back door every few seconds. Just enough to leave an evenly-spaced trail of splotches a few yards apart. Just enough to look deliberate.

Is there as simple an explanation for the dead bodies in the Delta? I can only hope.

CHAPTER SEVENTEEN

Clarice looks pale when I spot her through my office window coming into the newsroom. I wave her in and she nods, dropping her purse, phone and sunglasses on her desk before she looms in the door.

"You don't look so good. Tell me."

"I really don't want to do a story on this, Amy." Her voice is subdued.

"What is it?"

"She's in a coma. Her injuries are horrific."

"Did you get in to see her? I could only get confirmation that she'd been admitted."

She shakes her head. I know she has a strong stomach but she's fighting nausea. "No, I was able to look at the police report. That SOB beat her with a baseball bat. She has a broken leg, broken jaw, broken ribs and a fractured skull. That's why she's in a coma."

"My God! Will she make it?"

"The doctors told the cops they're 'cautiously optimistic'. Nobody's gonna talk to her until she's conscious."

"How'd she get to the hospital?"

Clarice blows out a breath. "Probably one of your ladies. A neighbor went over to ask Suzy if she wanted to go to the movies. Suzy's car was there, but her husband's truck wasn't so the neighbor thought it was a good time. She knocked on the door, called her and then went around the back to see if she was in the yard. The back door screen was banging. The neighbor grabbed it, went into the kitchen and found Suzy on the floor, covered in blood. She called 911, the police and paramedics showed up, the neighbor was interviewed and Suzy was rushed to the hospital."

If Clarice could get her hands on Suzy's husband, he wouldn't make it. And I'd like to tap dance on his face in stilettos. What could possibly make a man think he had the right to beat up...and maybe kill...a woman? A woman he'd promised to love and protect?

"Have they arrested the guy yet?"

"No. There's a BOLO for his truck. According to the neighbor, he's on Workers' Comp or some sort of disability and doesn't go very far from home. What's his disability? He was strong enough to swing a baseball bat."

Clarice goes silent. I wonder what she's thinking besides violence and mayhem to Suzy's husband. "On second thought, I do want to do this story. Not right now. I'll cover the SOB's arrest, but if Suzy's strong enough later, I'd like to tell her story. One thing I can do now is go out to her neighborhood. Talk to her friends. Maybe ask about the drilling crews. See if anybody links Suzy's beating with the murders."

I can see that Clarice has moved Suzy's husband into the top "Person of Interest" slot for any crime in the Delta...and possibly for a fifty-mile radius.

"Are you OK to head out there now?"

"I'm fine. I'll stop for a coffee. The caffeine should keep me until I can find someone to talk to. I want to do it now, while there's still a shock factor and before the rumors get so involved that nobody remembers what *really* happened."

"Call me." I know she will.

I call Nancy to ask if she's available for a few minutes of brainstorming. Not about Suzy and the beating, but if she's aware of any link between Posse members and domestic abuse. She's free and we meet at the coffee shop next to the library.

"I did a quick search. There are some assumed connections," she says as we stand in line for our iced lattes. The need for caffeine doesn't go away just because the temperature rises.

"The problem is that those people...the survivalists, the fringe right, the conspiracy folks...are all secretive. They don't trust any law enforcement so never call the cops. And they wouldn't take a gunshot victim to a hospital because of the reporting requirements."

What she doesn't mention is that no one seems to get away from these sects. Nobody leaves, looking for a million dollar media deal for a "tell-all" about being a member of an anti-government group. It may be brainwashing, it may be bone-chilling fear, but once a man...and it's almost always men who get involved...belongs, his family joins as well. If any women or kids get away from the group, they don't talk.

I don't understand the pervasive power of brainwashing. I was astounded when the Fundamentalist Church of Jesus Christ of Latter Day Saints, Warren Jeffs' sect, was exposed and Jeffs sentenced to life in prison for a "pervasion pattern" of sexual assault. Even from prison, Jeffs managed to keep some members of the sect, and some women, involved. Fact and logic don't stand a chance in the face of beliefs and faith.

"I haven't done a LexisNexis search for links." What I don't say is that I've been too wrapped up in water to look for right-wing groups. "Is it worthwhile getting Clarice to look?"

Nancy sucks on an ice cube from the bottom of her latte. I can see her brain working from her frown. "I wouldn't bother. You have an abuse victim, you've found her neighbors, and maybe friends. Whether or not her husband is involved with the conspiracy folks seems immaterial. When they arrest him for the assault, then's the time to dig deeper. If I run across anything, though, I'll call you."

She picks up her purse, hulas her hips to skirt around the other small tables and says, "Thanks for the coffee break. Wakes me up and cools me off!" With a finger wave, she's gone.

On the way back to the *Press*, my cell rings. Dodson's name pops up. I say, "This is A...." and before I can get my name out he says, "Can you come over to my office?"

"I'll be right there. Is there anything I should know?"

"We'll talk when you get here" and the phone goes dead.

Interesting. Jim Dodson isn't usually rude or secretive. Clarice? No, he would have mentioned her—wouldn't he? Speculating won't get me anywhere, a fast walk is better. Perspiration gathers at my hairline and the cooling effect of the latte is wearing off after my fast hike to his office.

His assistant's on the phone but waves me in. Two steps and I stop. He's not alone. Two men in suits stand up. Dodson says, "Amy, this is Lt. Laver Krutz and Lt. Harrison Wilkes of the California Highway Patrol." He waves at me. "And this is Amy Hobbes, Managing Editor of the Monroe *Press*."

The men nod and reach out hands. The one named Krutz says, "Nice to meet you," with his mouth but not his eyes. The other says, "Good to meet you. Please call me Harry." Before we even exchange greetings, I have good cop-bad cop.

Dodson has a small wrinkle at the edge of his right eye but his voice is smooth. "The Highway Patrol officers came down from Sacramento to talk about the BOLO on Gunther Mohre."

He watches my blank expression and adds, "Gunther Mohre is wanted for assaulting his wife."

So, Suzy's husband has a name.

CHAPTER EIGHTEEN

"**A**my is the one who overheard a conversation about a woman named Suzy who was a continuing victim of domestic violence. We watched for another domestic call. Without this recent assault, we may never have looked at Mohre in connection with the Freeland murders."

This is an interesting admission from our Sheriff. I debate the best way to play this. "Is Mohre a suspect in the murders?"

Krutz' mouth sucks on a sour lime. "If he were, we certainly wouldn't tell the press about it. We're here to ask you exactly what you heard."

Hoo, boy, I bet this guy gets invited to all the parties and has loads of friends. "I didn't think too much of it at the time. Two women were chatting while having their nails done. One of them said, 'Poor Suzy, that husband of hers smacked her around after she let the surveyor into their back yard'."

"That's it?" Krutz eyes me as though he'd like to get out the rubber hoses and truth serum.

"They talked a bit more about how Suzy needed to get rid of him."

"Did you say anything to them?"

"I said I was a journalist and wasn't it going to be a hot summer and where did they live? They said the Delta, picked up their stuff and left. I think it was the nosy journalist that spooked them."

"Just call me Harry" smiles at me...with his eyes yet. And nice milk chocolate ones they are, too. "Why did you think this was a conversation worth passing along to the Sheriff?"

"The mention of the surveyor. There are always surveys going on with all the new developments, but the only ones I know about in the Delta are for the tunnels. And there's a big 'Stop the Tunnels' movement in the Delta. And the two murder victims were killed in the Freeland corporation yard where the drilling equipment is housed. It seemed too much of a coincidence."

Dodson has been trying to use his X-ray vision to bore a hole in his desk during this. Odd, he's a stand-up guy and usually any of the outside agency people don't bother him. I glance at him again and realize he has a trace of a smile at the corner of his mouth. Maybe an X-ray is better than a laugh.

Now he raises his eyes, all business. "I'm glad you did, Amy. And these gentlemen are as well." He gestures to the two CHP officers and Krutz nods while Wilkes all but grins. "This hasn't led to anything, but you know that there's no such thing as coincidence."

I do know that. What looks like a coincidence from the outside becomes a logical sequence of events once the inside is explained. "Have you gotten any tips from the BOLO? Are you going to put it up on the freeway signs?"

CalTrans, responsible for all the freeways and highways in the state, began installing huge display signs a few years ago to issue Amber Alerts for missing or abducted children. Now they're used for a variety of information, including traffic problems or accidents, estimated times to various destinations, "Don't Drink and Drive" warnings and the occasional "Save Water" pleas. I've wondered how many tips get called in when the signs say "Light green Toyota, license plate 4XYZ blah, blah. Wanted for..."

"No." Krutz' answer is short and curt.

Harry adds, "This is pretty local. It began as a domestic and those guys don't pick up and leave. They think they're entitled to whatever they did. 'She pushed me to it.' It's never their fault. We're watching his house and he'll be back. We'd like to get him earlier rather than later, but we'll get him."

"All of this interest over a domestic that turned into an aggravated assault?" I'm thinking that Clarice could walk into a mess at the Mohre house.

Dodson looks a little pained and Harry says, "You said it yourself. It's too many coincidences. A violent man. Two bodies. Anger over a state project. We don't want to find a guy lashing out at everything. We're taking these warning signs seriously. Too many random shootings and attacks from 'that nice guy' have forced us to move fast and broadly when there's a possibility of someone going off the tracks. Particularly when there're priors involving violence."

I look at him. His brown eyes are serious, now, but I can see laugh crinkles on the outside edges. Harry Wilkes hasn't let the pressures and dangers of his job kill all his humanness. It's a nice admission from him. I know their hands are tied in many cases, even though they may suspect violence isn't far from the surface. School and workplace multiple shootings have stunned everybody and the population is demanding faster reaction to possible threats.

"Are you going to interview Suzy Mohre?" I look at Dodson with this question and cross my mental fingers that Krutz isn't heading to the hospital. His cold, gruff manner won't make a seriously injured battered woman open up to him.

"We have a deputy at the hospital now, and she'll call us as soon as the doctors feel Ms. Mohre is up to answering questions." Krutz stares at Dodson, seemingly appalled he'd share this with the press, and Dodson says, "Lt. Krutz, this may not be protocol for the Highway Patrol, but I've found that working with certain members of the press has been beneficial. I trust Amy. She understands confidential information."

I feel a warm spot growing in my chest. Sheriff Jim Dodson is one of the good guys and knows that we're on the same side—even though we go about getting and using information differently.

Clarice needs to handle him carefully; he's too caring to lose.

As I stand and say my goodbyes, my stomach rumbles, a bass counterpoint to the conversation. I don't eat breakfast and the latte only stayed for a bit.

On the sidewalk I skim through my options. It'll have to be a take-out, I spent enough time away from my office already. This is hard. I can decide in a heartbeat what stories to put on page one, but I stand in the growing heat raising and rejecting lunch choices.

A chicken Caesar salad finally gathers enough votes and I head for the deli two blocks away. I'm never incognito in public in Monroe. Either people recognize me from the paper or as Brandon's ex-wife. Two women eating lunch at an outside table wave and a guy in line for his food says, "Hey, Amy. How you doing?" This meeting and greeting isn't a bad thing although today I'm hungry and cranky and don't want to chat beyond a "how are you."

Back in the air conditioning of my office, I'm digging into the salad when Clarice calls. "Suzy is the focal point of her neighborhood out here." I can hear some heavy equipment in the background.

"Where's here?"

A sigh. "Where you sent me. Freeland. Can't you hear all the trucks?"

"I hear a lot of noise. What's going on?"

"They're moving all the drilling equipment around so it's covered by the surveillance cameras."

Seems a little late for that. "Is it because of the murders?"

Clarice says, "Pfffttt...no. I asked the guys and they said the company's worried about theft. I guess two dead workers aren't important."

There's an increase in the background noise, Clarice says, "Hey you guys, watch that..." then a crunching sound before the phone goes dead.

I yell, "Clarice, Clarice," sure that there's no phone at the other end. Is there Clarice, though?

CHAPTER NINETEEN

What the hell could have happened? Clarice was hit by a truck? Her car was rammed? Was she even in her car? She dropped her phone and it broke? Someone slugged her? I had visions of Gunther Mohre and his baseball bat.

Without thinking, I hit call back and it goes to nothing. This isn't good. Clarice is out there and I can't get in touch with her, there's a violent man running around, two dead bodies have already turned up. What have I done?

One thing I've done is lose my ability to think in an emergency.

I gather what calm I can find and call Jim Dodson. He'd said he had a loose tail on her. This seems to be a good time to make it a tight tail.

When I'm transferred to him, I run down what little I know...mostly, "I was talking to Clarice, she said 'Hey look out' and her phone went dead." After I've said it, it doesn't sound as dreadful as I'd imagined. There can be a bunch of simple reasons.

Thank god Dodson reacts quickly, finding out which deputy is closest to Clarice's location and paging him with instructions to check out the yard. He says he'll call me as soon as the deputy calls in.

It's only a few minutes of nail-biting time before my phone rings with an unfamiliar ringtone and number. Ordinarily I'd ignore it. With Clarice gone, I hit accept and Clarice's voice fills my ear. She's in fine form, using expletives I didn't know she knew.

"Those SOBs!" She's yelling but I don't dare hold my phone away from my ear. All the office could hear her rant.

"What happened, Clar? And don't shout, you're going to burst my eardrum."

She inhales, then I hear her breath leaking out like a half-filled balloon. "I told you they were moving the equipment? Well, a big idiot wasn't watching where his boom was swinging. I thought he was going to swing it right into my car so I got out to yell at him. That's when one of the other goons shoved me, my phone flew out of my hand and a big truck ran over it. How am I going to fill out an expense form for this? Can you get me another one?"

Trust Clarice to cut to the chase. "Are you hurt?"

"No. I stumbled a little, but never fell down. And my phone would be OK if it hadn't made like a Hail Mary football."

I stifled a laugh. Even in trying times, Clarice can manipulate the language. "What were you doing in the corporation yard, anyway? I thought you were talking to Suzy's friends and neighbors."

"I was. I have been. One of the neighbors, a burly older guy, said her husband, Gunther—did you know his name is Gunther?"

"Just learned that from the Sheriff." I could almost keep up with her information stream.

"Anyway, Gunther is out on disability. He was a trucker. The neighbor," and now I hear shuffling notebook pages, "Mark Cruz, thinks he may be faking it. Cruz said Gunther still does some work around the house, drinks in the backyard, takes his boat out. He keeps to himself, has a nasty temper...threatened another neighbor over a barking dog."

"Did Cruz say Gunther has been around?"

After a brief silence, "No." I know she started to shake her head then realized I couldn't see her. "No one's seen his truck since Suzy was beaten up."

"So you went to the corporation yard, why?"

"Sometimes truckers stick together. I was hoping that one of these guys," and now I imagine her arm waving around to include everyone in a hundred-yard radius, "would know him. No such luck. They'd seen him out in his back yard drinking beer and were envious. Looked like a life they'd like."

"What phone are you using now? Is your car OK?"

"I'm using one of the deputy's. He got here awfully fast. Did you call the Sheriff?"

Clarice may not have majored in math, but she can put two and two together fast. "I did, yes. But mostly...." Now she's pissed and talking over me.

"Amy, don't you trust me? Why'd you send somebody to rescue me? I'm not a damsel in distress!"

"Of course I trust you, Clar. You have to know that it sounded ominous when your phone just went dead. I tried to call you back, but nothing."

"Right, nothing! It was under the wheels of a huge truck!"

"Clarice, for all I knew *you* were under the wheels."

"Well, I wasn't! And I could have used one of these guys' phones, or walked a couple of blocks and used a neighbor's phone. Good Lord, Amy, it's broad daylight and I'm surrounded by homes and stores." There's a lull in the rant, then "Oh my god, Amy, you called the Sheriff! I'm mortified! He's going to think I'm a great big sissy. How could you?"

I sense this isn't the best time to tell her Jim Dodson and I have agreed his folks need to keep an eye on her.

"Relax, he just patched through to the deputy closest to the corporation yard. No big deal." I put my hand up to see how far my nose had grown. "Your car's OK?"

"It's fine. Unless you have something else, I'm gonna finish talking to a few more people out here. I'd like to know more about Gunther Mohre and his disability."

"But you don't have a phone..."

"Amy, a lot of people don't have cell phones and the world gets along fine. I'm talking, I'm writing notes. I'll probably be out here another hour or so."

That'll give me time to figure out how to fill out an expense report that will fly past the publishers and get her set up with a new phone. When I took this job, I didn't think I'd be writing much fiction. Sometimes, though...

By the time she rolls into the office, I have a new phone for her and haven't sold my soul to Max and Calvin, the publishers. They're not happy, but do see the necessity.

"What else have you found?" I'm multi-tasking, scrolling through the budget to find page one stories while half my mind is listening.

"General agreement that Gunther Mohre is a pain. The women won't go near him because of the way he beats Suzy, and the men are leery because they think he's running a disability scam."

"Uh huh."

"One guy, that Mark Cruz, said it wouldn't surprise him if Mohre was involved in the murders."

At this, my attention zips from the budget on my screen. "What? He thinks Mohre's a murderer?"

Clarice's patience, never her long suit, wears out. "No, he doesn't think Mohre's a murderer. It just wouldn't surprise him. Mohre's violent and has lashed out at neighbors as well as taking it out on Suzy. There was an incidence last year when he came barreling out of his house swinging a baseball bat, yelling at a girl who'd let her dog wander onto his front lawn. The girl was terrified, ran home to tell her Dad, Dad arrived with a rifle, a lot of name-calling and threats were thrown, until one of the other neighborhood guys said, 'I'm calling the cops.' Things calmed down fast after that. These people don't want the cops nosing around."

"Why? It's sounding like the Wild West out there."

"No, just farmers." She gives me a funny look.

"Why do farmers walk around swinging baseball bats and rifles?"

She clears her throat. "I think it's because of crops they're growing."

A light begins to flash in my brain.

CHAPTER TWENTY

"**Y**ou think they're growing a 'cash crop'?" Clarice picks up on the air quotes in my voice.

She smiles. "I think that's exactly what they're growing. At least that's part of their crops, probably the part that gives them the most cash."

Marijuana has been a cash crop in California for more than forty years and it's the economic underpinning of a few rural Northern California counties. Now that it's legal to sell medical marijuana, the growers have become more open. In many of the urban areas, they've bought newer tract houses and turned entire structures into indoor gardens. Police and DEA raids aren't the only cost of doing business, there's a big threat from theft and more people are guarding their "farms" with thugs, guns and dogs.

The farmers in the Delta might not be growing acres, but even a few plants could yield enough money for them to keep an eye out for strangers.

"That would certainly make them nervous if any cops show up." I'm turning this over, looking for fractures and flaws when Clarice says, "Now Suzy makes sense."

"How so?"

"She only reported the beatings that left her scared. She knew if she called the cops, or if Gunther got pulled in, she'd get beaten worse when he came home. And for sure, letting a surveyor into the back yard, where he could have spotted the plants, was tantamount to telling law enforcement what was going on. No wonder he damned near killed her this time."

Clarice and I look at each other. This is beginning to look like an onion...every time we peel off a layer thinking we've reached the core, there's another layer. More pungent then the last.

"Do you want to call Sheriff Dodson?"

She sighs. "I should. I suspect they know about the growers out there. Those guys are just small time ones, though."

"Better to have this conversation with the Sheriff than to let that CHP guy bust it up."

"What CHP guy?" Her frown lines deepen then I realize that I haven't told her about Wilkins and Krutz. Her flying phone chased them from my mind. I do a quick recap of our meeting and she shakes her head.

"I'm glad that those guys are taking all this random murder and mayhem seriously. Almost every one of those mass shooters have had some signs that things aren't right with them. The Mohres' neighbors think he's too tightly wound. Are they going to interview Suzy?"

"If they do, I hope it's Wilkins. Krutz is as empathic as a dead flounder," a line that elicits a short snort from Clarice.

There may be some karmic forces at work because her new cell rings, she says, "Clarice here. Yeah? Oh yeah!" shoves it in her bag and makes for the door.

"Wait a minute!" I'm not looking managerial as I try to catch her. "What's going on."

"That was my pal at the hospital. Suzy is awake. I need to get there before the cops close off access to her," and she's gone.

This is the story that Clarice initially didn't want to write. Now, though, it may be fitting into a much larger piece of investigative work. She can bring in the drug angle, the two bodies in the corporation yard, possible disability fraud— there are plenty of ingredients boiling under the seemingly placid surface of the Delta. It's not yet clear which are tasty pieces of steak and which are spit-it-out gristle, but the meal is going to be Clarice's for the taking. Or else.

There's a lull since she bolted for the hospital and I take the opportunity to do more follow-up on the demolishing house in my neighborhood. I do a search on as many sites as I can and one lands a substantial trail. The name of the absentee Arizona owner is Oscar Munoz and the reason he hasn't paid the taxes is that he's doing a fifteen-to-thirty in an Arizona state penitentiary for trafficking—as a member of one of the Mexican cartels.

I sit back, roads of information building a spider web in my head. None of it yields a solid picture, but there are some recurring themes. Well, just one major one and it's drugs. The DEA keeps an eye on this part of California. Major east-west and north-south interstates cross just a few miles north in Sacramento, which leads to ease of distribution. Add in that this valley is home to major meth production and we're a target-rich environment.

If the house was used to grow, or manufacture...or even to process what was grown in the Delta, the DOJ could have seized it in an asset raid. And if it had been a meth manufacturing facility, it would have been so toxic that it had to be demolished.

A shiver of nerves shimmies down my spine. I pride myself on being aware and noticing my surroundings. What was probably some kind of drug house existed in my neighborhood and I didn't see it. Although to be fair, it had been operating for a while and nobody else noticed it, either. Not even the DEA.

I type up a longish note for the file. Right now, it's just an interesting little story, not important enough to do much with. It could become glue, though, that accumulation of facts, rumor and stories that tie together and make a bigger package.

In my head I'm turning pieces over and over, seeing what might fit and I jump when my cell rings. It's Clarice and it's iffy news.

"Suzy was awake when I got here. The worst-case scenario happened." She sounds disgusted.

"What's that?"

"One of the CHP guys showed up. It wasn't Wilkes. Boy, I see what you mean. Krutz walked in, kicked me out, slammed the door—which doesn't really slam, you know those pneumatic hospital doors, and that pissed him off even more—posted a deputy outside and said no one gets in to see her."

The frustration comes out as sarcasm, but I can't blame her. This was something we'd dug up ourselves. Chances are that law enforcement would put the stories together as fast as we did but I was the one who eavesdropped on the conversation in the nail salon.

In my mind it was newsgathering, that penchant for watching, listening and observing. It wasn't lost on me that a lot of people would call it nosy. We never set out to solve crimes, we were interested in the reasons for human behavior so we could tell the story.

"Did you get to talk to her?"

"Briefly." I'm hearing Clarice open her car door.

"Are you heading in to the office?"

"I'm going to swing by the Sheriff's office first. If the CHP guy is occupied with Suzy, it might be a good time to check up on the hunt for Mohre." A tick of silence, then, "And ask him if he's got a guard on me."

Hmmm, my explanation of why the deputy showed up so soon in Freeland only slowed her. I should know it wouldn't stop her. She's proud of her abilities and a bit heedless about getting into jams that could become dangerous. I don't want anything to happen because I'd assigned her to cover, or to dig up, a story.

It was hard enough to live with the guilt of having Vinnie die, even though I hadn't sent him into that high-speed chase. He was doing that scary job because he felt responsible for Heather and me. Never again did I want to be involved in anyone being hurt because of my actions.

CHAPTER TWENTY-ONE

I'm on the phone with Heather, engrossed in last-minute details for the coming weekend, when Clarice looms outside my office. I wave her in and she slumps in one of the chairs in front of my desk. She's already dumped her phone, purse and sunglasses in her own cubicle but has a death grip on her notebook.

"Gotta go, sweetie, see you Friday night," I say and click Heather off.

My eyebrows are almost meeting and Clarice sees the question.

"Why did you guys do it, Amy? Jim...Sheriff Dodson..." She's read my twitch at her use of his first name. "He told me that you'd asked him to 'keep an eye' on me."

From her tone, she's not angry, she's very hurt.

"I'm nervous about this, Clarice. It's not as though I don't trust you, I'd have done the same with any reporter. If there's some connection to the Posse, or to any of the right-wing hate groups, this could turn lethal."

She's not liking my reaction. "You know as well as I do that it's shaping up as a drug deal."

"If your theory's right, then explain the two murdered guys."

"They spotted Mohre working on his plants."

I'm quiet for a heartbeat. If Mohre is growing in any volume, he wouldn't want anyone either tipping off the cops or hatching a plan to harvest his crop for themselves.

"That's a little thin, Clarice. How much money are you guessing those plants would bring?"

"I don't know. Maybe fifty thousand? It would probably depend on how they distributed it."

My neighborhood drug house pops up in internal-vision. If they were cooking meth they could also have been growing and been a distribution center. A pharmaceutical enterprise in the middle of suburbia.

"You may have something." I fill Clarice in on the owner and use of the house around the corner.

Now she's the devil's advocate. "If it's drugs, where are the DEA guys? And if the owner is in Arizona, they have some rabid right wing nuts there."

Her eyes close and from the expressions fleeting across her face she's testing and rejecting ideas. Suddenly her eyes snap open.

"How do the right-wing groups fund themselves? Some of them have built compounds and seriously armed themselves. Who buys the land? Who pays for the builders? How do they feed themselves?"

All good questions. I have no answers. I take a stab. "The same way the cults do? Take all the members' money? Require them to recruit more members?"

Clarice is shaking her head. "If they're so isolated, how do members go out to recruit? And where? Gun shows? These aren't the kind of groups that hold protest marches or pot lucks."

"You're headed somewhere with this, Clarice. Let's stop the Twenty Questions. What's up?"

She drums her fingers on my desk. Begins to hum. Her eyes are focused on something deep in her head. She usually has her thoughts close to the surface and uses several "tells" that make it easy to understand her. Now, she's pulling from the back of her brain.

"We keep adding things. First the killings. Then the 'Stop the Tunnels' crowd. Then Suzy. Then the CHP. Then the crops. Then your drug house. Then the connection to the cartels. What if they're not separate events? What if they're tied together somehow?"

I look at her. She may have a point. "But how? The Mexican drug cartels are behind the 'Stop the Tunnels' movement? Because they don't want the state to find their crops? That doesn't make any sense, Clarice. The amount of weed that's growing in the Delta isn't even a drop in the bucket of drugs that come cross the border."

She gives me one of her looks. "Amy, I didn't say there's a direct correlation. It's just that suddenly the Delta, a sleepy area of small farms, small towns, small fishing resorts, small boat marinas, is the focus of what might be California's biggest infrastructure projects ever. Lot of eyes out there. Maybe enough to make some people nervous."

Small boat marinas? I grab that. "Wait a minute, the marinas. The Delta connects to San Francisco Bay. Do we know about any smuggling that happens there? The traffic into Florida by boat is huge, all those cigarette boats outrunning the Coast Guard. What about smaller sailboats, smaller yachts, even fishing boats coming up the river?"

After I've blurted it out, I have second thoughts. The boats that pull into the marinas on the Delta aren't big enough to hold quantities of drugs to make it worthwhile, but I like the way she's thinking. I'm sure there's a link that ties this all together. We're silent, then I say "Suzy?" As a Eureka moment, it's pretty lame, but Clarice brightens.

"Suzy."

"Did you get a chance to talk to her before Krutz stomped in?"

"I did."

"Well?"

She shakes her head and takes a breath. "I just got the beginnings of her story. When they were first married, Gunther was an OK guy. He drove truck for the companies in this area that cover the state. He'd get a few long-haul contracts, but mostly he did runs back and forth to LA or Oregon. He wasn't gone for days at a time. Eventually, he bought his own rig and started taking on long-hauls. They bought a house near Tracy and were doing fine. She got lonely. They bought in one of those new tracts that are going in. Didn't know anyone and most of her neighbors were gone all day at work so she took a part-time clerical job at a distribution center."

I pick up a pen and start jotting notes. All this background is fine, but we need some action. I'm aware that Gwen has walked by my office, slowly, twice and glanced in. She hasn't interrupted even though I know she needs to talk to me.

"Clar, you aren't going to do anything with this for tomorrow, right? Let's keep talking."

She looks up from where she's been flipping notebook pages, focuses on where she is. "No, no, that's fine. I still have the hospital source who'll let me know when the gorillas go off guard duty." Standing, she moves back to her desk to transcribe her notes. Something has gotten to her, but I have a paper to put out and whatever it is will have to wait a bit.

I wave Gwen in, she takes the chair that Clarice just vacated and says, "Well, the proverbial stuff has hit the fan. A group called STOUT has formed and filed a suit against the city over the Harvest of Praise."

Just when you think it's safe to walk outside. "STOUT? What the heck is that?" Gwen's not a goodie-goodie but I try and watch my mouth around her.

"Stop Taking Our Taxes," she says. "They played a little lose with the acronym because they wanted the visual of feeding from the public trough."

"Just what are they accusing the city of? A lot of people were upset at the placement and zoning for this project, but as far as I know there isn't any public money in it. It's private. It's a church, for heaven's sake."

Gwen pulls a sheaf of papers that look a lot like a legal filing out of a folder. "It's private and it's a church," she acknowledges. "There are two complaints in here. First, because the use as a church takes the land off the tax rolls, the city and county lose money and secondly..." She pauses for a dramatic revelation. "The city has agreed to put some money in."

"What! They've gone crazy! People will never stand for public money going to support a private church!" I may be on the verge of yelling, but I'm truly speechless. Could the city leaders be that dense?

CHAPTER TWENTY-TWO

According to the lawsuit, a copy of which Gwen picked up from the City Attorney's office, they could be that dense. It's not as overt as actually funding part of the construction, but they have agreed to widen the streets, reroute some traffic patterns, put in left-hand turn lanes and install signals at either end of the block where the project will sit. A significant change for traffic patterns in that neighborhood.

"Did the anti-church people know this was happening?" I can't believe the project got this far without someone pulling the plug.

Gwen wrinkles her nose. Maybe she smells the rat? "It was never spelled out. The full proposal said the church group would pay for traffic engineering studies on the possible impact. It wasn't until the traffic engineers took a look that all the changes became clear and could be costed out. The church people said those were permanent city improvements and they shouldn't have to pay for them, the city agreed and presto! It's a small item in the city works budget."

This mega-church is never going to go away. It's bad enough that one of the councilmembers is also a ranking Harvest of Praise member. He recused himself from any votes on the issue, but that didn't stop him from buttonholing all the other councilmembers, as well as the area movers and shakers, to tout this.

According to Gwen, who's covered most of this for months, he developed the argument that even though the land was off the tax rolls, the complex was a boost to the local economy. "His standard line was that all of the activity at the church, and maybe the 'Education Center,' was helpful. It would create jobs and people using the facilities would shop and eat locally. It would bring in people from outside Monroe, and capture some of their spending."

I just stare at her. "So the Harvest of Praise people used the 'economic multiplier effect'?" This is a plank that boosters of the arts and sports venues use in their arguments, along with the "It's clean industry" line.

I know I'm having a hard time closing my mouth around this. "So a church is now a non-polluting business?"

She nods.

"How has this gotten so far along? Didn't Dennis Roberts come across this?" Roberts is the religion reporter and for him the word "investigation" ended with the Shroud of Turin.

Gwen is too much of a lady to call Roberts a flake, but we both know this isn't information he would have come across. His usual sources are the leadership and parishioners of the local churches. Even getting him to do a story on the Jewish temple—let alone the Muslim mosque—in town, requires constant pushing and threats of putting him on the obits beat.

"For him to uncover this, he'd have to know the city's budget and where to look. I glanced over it when they presented it and didn't spot it. It'll be voted on in two weeks.

I'm just happy that somebody from the anti crowd could read and understand the budget." Gwen gives a little shiver.

Hmmm, what's she telling me? "Are you against the project?" Reporters have to maintain as much objectivity as possible because they tell all sides of the story. That doesn't mean they have no preferences or biases themselves.

"No, not against it, exactly. I think it's too big a project for the area it's sited on. I'm interested because of the machinations some people in town have gone through to make sure it's approved and built. It's a good story with legs and now this...possible collusion between some of the city leaders and the church leaders."

Collusion? She's right, this can make a very nice package, looking at who pulls the strings and makes the decisions.

"You've got this, Gwen. Don't let your regular work suffer. If you feel overwhelmed, let me know and I'll get an intern to cover routine city meetings. For tomorrow, a small page one story is good. Just enough information to let everyone know we'll be calling them, sooner rather than later."

She smiles at me and nods again. Have I let my interactions with Clarice become so engrossing that I've overlooked a solid, competent, able reporter? I've always liked Gwen and feel we work well together. Now I'm pleased that she's dug up something that can make a difference.

As she heads out to her desk, I do a silent whoop of happiness. I have two great reporters working on two in-depth stories and no other media in the area knows about them. Old-fashioned, but can you say scoop?

The early evening grinds down as the reporters file their stories and the copy desk designs the pages. There's a contented low hum in the newsroom of clacking keys and writers winding up the final calls.

By seven, everything's wrapped up and I head for the grocery store to stock up for the weekend. Heather's tastes have morphed from macaroni and cheese to brie and imported crackers with a good bottle of a Sonoma County Chardonnay. More expensive, but it's nice to have a grown-up daughter to share this with. I wouldn't buy these things for myself because they go bad faster than I can eat or drink them.

Cleaning, changing sheets, finishing laundry, putting flowers in Heather's room and the dining room take up my evening. I know the bouquets are just grocery-store, but there's a feeling of small luxury and finesse that come with the splurge.

Mac and I do our evening walk, each of us immersed in our thoughts. I'm pretty sure his revolve around "who's been there" and mine are "what's next?" Just one more difference. He's about an hour in the past and I'm trying to control the future.

I think he wins at this.

I'm tired but a little jazzed. My daughter's coming home, I'm spending next weekend with Phil and I have two projects at work that will keep my attention and take up my time. Once in my jammies—an old t-shirt from a concert that Heather went to when she was in high school—I log on and start writing notes to myself.

Gwen will probably spend a few hours tomorrow going through the city budget. Kenny, the guy who gave her the tip, can help her frame any questions, then she'll have to talk to the city manager, some councilmembers, the pastor and a couple of the board members of the church. She'll also need to talk to the anti- people and the attorney who filed the suit.

The full story may not even run for a week or so. It should be before the council takes their final vote on the budget and that meeting will be interesting. Usually by the time the budget gets to this point, all involved have had their say and the last vote is just a rubber stamp. This year, there may be fireworks after this story hits the streets.

Ah, anticipation.

And then there's Clarice, Suzy, Gunther, the CHP and maybe druggies. What a spicy cauldron. The first thing I have to do tomorrow is take Clarice off somewhere quiet and hear the rest of Suzy's story.

If I have to get my adrenaline second hand, it works with stories like these where there's enough to go around. I still have a twinge of remorse that I'm not out on the front lines any more. I comfort myself with the knowledge that I'm giving both Gwen and Clarice room and time to explore and making sure I have their backs with the rest of the staff.

It makes me crazy that a room full of grownups can still play "Mom always likes you best."

CHAPTER TWENTY-THREE

Finding quiet time to get Clarice away looks problematic the next morning. She has information, I can see it in her preoccupied stares at her notebook, her glances at her computer screen and her frown when she catches my eye. Every time she starts to head into my office, one of us is dragged away by the phone.

After the last one, a note pops up, "just heard from Suzy. coast is clear. heading to hospital again." By the time I hang up my most recent call and turn to look, her cubicle is empty.

Gwen is heading my way, so I put the Suzy problem out of the way and clear my mind for the looming city budget scandal.

"Have a minute?" Gwen's pleasant question doesn't make my skin shiver like Clarice's mid-stream-of-consciousness jolt does when she realizes where she is. Even though Clarice knows she's coming into my office, she always gives a start as though she's found herself in unknown territory.

"Sure, come on in." I wave at the chair in front of my desk, clear of rubble this early in the day, and pick up a pen.

I find it's good to have a prop, something mindless to do with my hands as I let the stories sink into my brain.

We've had some blowback already from the small story this morning—the topic of most of my phone calls—but the full impact hasn't hit yet.

"What have you heard?" Gwen seems a tad nervous, she's crossed her legs and her free foot is tapping against my desk.

"So far, I've gotten calls from the city manager, one councilmember and two of our finest conspiracy theorists who said, 'I told you so!' What have you heard?"

"About the same. Two of the church members called me, one of them in tears. She asked why we were so opposed to the church expansion that we'd print lies. I told her they weren't lies, just line items in the city's budget and that we were going to continue to look into it. She hung up on me."

We look at each other. We knew yesterday, when Gwen found the line in the budget for the street "improvements" that we weren't going to be popular. Sometimes it's tough to live in a place where you have to turn over an occasional rock and show the slime. Both of us believe that's it's a necessary job we do, no matter how uncomfortable.

In the next quarter-hour, we sketch out the list of folks to call and develop a beginning frame to the story. We need to raise questions, not just tar with a broad brush.

The councilmember on the church board did recuse himself from voting on the project, but what did he know and when did he know it? Did he "drop in" to the traffic engineering department to look at the proposed traffic flow? He sits on the council's budget committee, did he have a chance to analyze the construction costs?

And she needs to talk to the traffic engineer who looked at the current and proposed patterns. Will the widening and additional stop signs or lights disrupt traffic anywhere else in the neighborhood?

Maybe I need to talk to the mayor and some others and work up an editorial. I'm interested in why the Chamber of

Commerce has bought into the argument that this is a clean way to increase business.

I jot some notes, Gwen heads off to begin her phone calls. I can hear her setting up a lunch meeting with the councilmember. Talking with a source in a social setting can be iffy. Some people jump to the conclusion that all is friendly and feel betrayed when a story doesn't put them in the best light. On the other hand, sharing a meal can bridge the assumption that the source is being grilled.

Clarice is back a bit after noon and she has the cat with the cream look. When she strolls into my office, I ask, "Have you eaten?"

The topic causes her to stop and frown. When she's on the trail, she's single-minded and I've known her to skip meals. She may be using it as a weight-loss tactic, but I know she also gets cranky without food...not pleasant to work with.

"No, I left the hospital when they were bringing in lunch. Are you buying?"

"Sure." I pull my purse out of the drawer, take one quick look at e-mail. "What sounds good?"

"It's heating up, how about the new pub place? It's cool and dark inside."

This is a good choice. Although it's becoming the chi-chi place to lunch, we can get a table in the back and avoid some prying eyes and ears.

Once we've ordered, I say "Spill" as she says, "Well..." With Clarice, I don't have to pry information out.

"Suzy has a kind of typical battered woman story, but there's a little twist."

Suzy Mohre became depressed at her inability to get pregnant. She and Gunther hadn't really discussed children, but she just knew Gunther would be happy if she was carrying his child. She lulled herself to sleep nights with visions of an adorable little girl who she could dress up and who would follow her around, learning to cook and clean just as she did.

Clarice looks up from her notebook. "Suzy said she didn't care, a boy, a miniature version of Gunther would be fine. She got pretty dreamy when she was telling me this."

Gunther would teach the boy how to throw a ball and how to work on engines and Suzy would have two males to remind about wiping their feet off and washing their hands of the oil and grease before eating. It would be more work for her, but the love would far surpass the tasks.

They'd been married half a dozen years when Gunther came home and announced he'd bought some land in the Delta near the tiny town of Freeland. They were moving.

"When was this?" I knew not many people moved to the Delta because any construction or renovation required a ton of permits.

Clarice pages through her notes. "This was about five years ago. They'd been living in Tracy. Gunther was a trucker and bought his own rig to do long-haul jobs. Suzy said she was lonely, living in Freeland with him gone so much, but there was enough land for her to start a garden. She sold her tomatoes, squash, and other stuff at a roadside stand beside their mailbox."

I close my eyes, picturing, then they snap open. "I know where her stand is...or was. I bought tomatoes there once." It centers me, being able to visualize how these pieces fit together.

Suzy was worried. Gunther was gone a lot and when he was home, he spent time with two other guys who owned small plots of land near them. He came home one day with a box of seedlings from one of the neighbors and told her he was planting them in her patch of corn. He'd never paid any attention to her garden until now.

The day she accidently chopped one of his plants down when weeding the corn was the first time he hit her. He came stomping in the kitchen with the bedraggled plant, threw it on her clean kitchen floor and slapped her across her face so hard that she bounced against a cabinet before hitting the floor.

Clarice isn't comfortable telling this story, even to me. "He used to call her a cow, told her how stupid she was. Threatened her that she better not touch any of his plants again."

I blow out a breath. "Well, if he was growing, he wouldn't want her to talk about it."

"True." Clarice taps a finger on her lip then smooths her eyebrow. She's seriously uncomfortable and I have a sudden thought about her background. We've never talked about it, but maybe there was some abuse? "The beatings got really bad when Gunther went on disability."

I frown. "Odd, I'd thought with money coming in he'd ease up a bit."

"No, I think this was just the last straw that proved his loser status. Couldn't even keep his job...or his truck."

CHAPTER TWENTY-FOUR

Clarice's voice gets more quiet as she continues her story. Apparently, over the past couple of years Gunther lost all control over his anger

He'd hit Suzy if he came home and dinner wasn't ready. He'd lie in wait for her if she was out and rail at her when she came home, battering her with questions about where she'd been and who she talked to.

No matter what her answer, he'd grab her arm and sling her against a piece of furniture or punch her in the stomach or chest, taking some care so that her bruises didn't show. After that first time, he seldom hit her in the face.

She stopped going out when he was home, choosing those times when he was gone for her shopping or visiting with neighbors. Once, drinking iced tea with a neighbor, the woman noticed a large bruise on her shoulder. Suzy hadn't thought, and wore a sleeveless blouse on the warm day, but seeing the woman's eyes, she said she'd banged into the kitchen door while carrying a full basket of tomatoes.

After that, she dressed carefully any time she left the house, even to work at her vegetable stand.

"Wait a minute, you found domestic violence calls to the Sheriff's Department. Did Suzy call the cops?"

Clarice gives me a funny look. "Of course not. She wouldn't dare. It was the neighbors who called, every time."

That made sense. Suzy wouldn't have wanted her shame to be public, but she couldn't contain the noise of Gunther's rages. "Why didn't the cops arrest him before this?"

"They took him in a few times to let him 'cool down', but Suzy would never press charges. She always had an explanation for her bruises and the broken furniture."

"Why this time? Isn't there a BOLO out on his truck?"

"Two things. First, the neighbor found her unconscious on her kitchen floor and second, they found all the plants growing in the corn. Even if you have a contract with a medically-approved dealer, Gunther had more than a hundred plants. He was over the line on this one."

I pictured that small farm stand and dimly saw the woman who was selling her home-grown produce. There wasn't anything in the picture that bothered me...nothing that hinted at the violence and fear that was Suzy's life. I know that domestic violence isn't confined to any demographic, any economic strata, any education level. Seeing that snapshot of quiet Delta life jolts me somehow.

"How long will she be in the hospital?"

"Probably another couple of days." Clarice taps her fork against her plate, just one of her nervous tells. Something is eating at her.

"Where are you on this?"

She pulls her eyes up and looks at me. "I'm worried. Suzy is going to need a long healing time. She'll probably have some casts on for weeks and won't be able to take care of herself." A pause, then "And I don't want to see her going back to her house...ever."

This isn't the time or place, but I know that I'm going to have to pull Clarice's story out, even if it's in small bits. She's such a good reporter because she's empathic with her sources and interviews, but she has a stronger reaction to Suzy than to anyone I've seen.

I pick up the check and root through my wallet, this commonplace action giving me a chance to marshal my thoughts. "Well, where can she go? Do any of the shelters have room?"

"I haven't checked yet. Most of them are designed for women with children and she needs more help than they can give her. She can't manage crutches with her broken ribs and the break in her femur had to be put together with screws and a plate. She'll be off it for at least six weeks. That means she's immobile." Clarice is giving off Eeyore vibes, clouds of woe seeping out. Is she looking to me for answers? I hope not, because I don't have any.

As she picks up her purse, she mumbles something. I catch "my house."

"What?"

"I guess she'll have to stay at my house."

I'm paralyzed. Clarice lives in a small one-bedroom apartment. She's gone most of every day. Her budget won't stretch to feed another person. Not to mention the problem of ethics. Suzy is the source for a story on domestic violence as well as a witness in a criminal investigation.

"Have you lost your mind?" I rattle off my objections and hammer home the ethics. "I'd have to pull you off the stories, including whatever's going on in the Delta. Now that we know Gunther's growing, the CHP will peg him as a person of interest. No...no, no, can't happen."

"Well, what can I do, Amy? The hospital will release her this week and she has to have a place to stay."

My brain is running down the list of charities and facilities that help victims and I say, "Talk to the social worker at the hospital and get Suzy in touch with Victim Witness. You can visit her once she's settled somewhere, but she's not going to be your houseguest."

I have a moment of sadness as we push through the restaurant doors back into the heat. Clarice's heart is in the right place. I wait until we're on the sidewalk before I say, "Clar, I'm not trying to be nosy, but why this protectiveness of Suzy?"

She swivels her eyes to me and slams her shades on as I notice moisture gathering. "It brings back memories," she says. "And before you jump to conclusions, it wasn't me. It was my best friend and next-door neighbor. Her dad beat up her mom and when Angie was about six, he started on her. Eventually, a teacher at school noticed Angie's bruises, Child Protective Services got involved, Angie got put in a foster home and then one night her dad beat her mom to death.

"Angie stayed in the foster system until she was eighteen and then I lost track of her. We were going to go to college together, share a dorm room, but she had nobody to help her out. She got a job at a plant that made parts for mobile homes and our lives just separated."

Oh, wow. I sit around licking my wounds from having my husband run off with another woman. Tiny, tiny potatoes compared to what Clarice witnessed.

"I had no idea, Clar. That's an awful story. Do you know where Angie is now?"

She shakes her head. "Nope. I'm guessing she's still in some small Midwest town, working at a dead-end job. When I called the company she was working for, they said she'd quit but didn't have a forwarding address."

"Have you looked online? People can't hide much any more."

"No. It hurts too much," she says, hitching her bag higher on her shoulder and picking up her pace.

CHAPTER TWENTY-FIVE

I turn for the office and Clarice heads for the city police and sheriff's offices. She'll look for routine calls and see where the hunt for Gunther stands. I'm sure she'll try and pin down the CHP guys, Krutz and "Just call me Harry," but doubt they'll give up much.

Gwen is on the phone...still...and there's a blizzard of pink notes drifting across my desk, all of which say "IMPORTANT". Of course. Sorting them by times gives me three increasingly strident notes from the Chamber of Commerce exec, two from the church's congregation president and four from neighbors.

This is why they pay me the big bucks...not!

I hit the Chamber's number and close my eyes. I'm making bets with myself about the tack he'll take so I'm surprised when his voice comes through in all reasonableness.

"Hi Amy, thanks for returning my call," he says. Hmmm, I wonder if waiting for a couple of hours calmed him down. Did I inadvertently end up playing a small power game?

"What can I help you with, Art?"

"Well, I've been hearing things on the grapevine that you and Gwen are looking at the church project. I thought this was cut and dried. Why are you bringing it up again?"

His tone is reasonable, but there's anger and venom behind it. Who's using him as a mouthpiece? "The project has certainly gone through the process and a ton of folks have had their say. Traffic mitigation is one of the issues, but no one ever talked about who would pay for it."

I can hear a faint snort. "Well, since it's city streets, I would have thought it was clear that the city would pay for it."

That's a spurious argument and he knows it. If the cost to the city had come up in any of the public hearings, there would have been outrage that the city—e.g. all the residents—were paying for street work that benefitted one project, a church.

"Art, what's the Chamber's interest in this? I don't remember that you've gone to bat for any other church."

There's a thick silence, then, "It's not the fact that it's a church, Amy. It's a big construction project with lots of jobs. Once it's up, locals will be hired for maintenance. The church and school staff will live in town and be part of the economy. They have several different-sized rooms for weddings and other events and they're planning to bring in touring Christian music groups."

"Fine, I can see where they have plans to keep the facility in full use. But how does that help the economy?" Am I being deliberately obtuse about this? No matter how I turn it, I don't see the money.

"Do you have any idea how big those Christian music tours are? They fill huge auditoriums."

"I just don't see that many people in Monroe going to those concerts on any regular basis."

Now he blows out a breath of exasperation. "Amy, they're planning this as a regional draw. They plan to advertise these things from Sacramento to Fresno, to the Bay

Area. They're basing their marketing on a demographic of five or six million people, with the largest population of conservative, mainstream Christians in the state. These people are savvy."

This makes me sit up straight. I'd never thought about a Christian performing arts center. Could something like this work? This is the "clean industry" argument that builders of performing arts centers and sports arenas have successfully used before. I'm beginning to see why the Chamber has glued itself to this project.

"So you're thinking of all the spill-over benefits. Restaurants, motels, travel needs..."

"You're seeing the vision, now, Amy. Down the line they're planning to put in an RV park and there's been some talk of a theme park."

I had no idea this was in the works. No wonder they want the infrastructure in place before they start on their long-range plan. "Is the city aware of these plans?"

"If you mean have they filed even preliminary prezoning documents, no not yet. This is still very much in the wish stages." Art is backpedaling on his Chamber persona now, nervous that he's let slip some very private plans.

"Is there a timeframe for all of this? It's an ambitious undertaking."

Art's voice is all business. "This is all off the record, Amy. I'm not really part of the planning group, I just know they're looking down the road. They want to have all their ducks in a row with a project this big."

Looking down the road? Ducks in a row? Art can slam into cliche-speak faster than almost anybody I've met.

"Thanks for the background, Art. I had no idea the project was so encompassing."

He clears his throat. "Um, hmmm, what are you going to do on this? Will you be writing an editorial? We'd sure like the *Press* to be in favor of it, it's an economic shot in the arm for Monroe."

I clench my teeth at the buzzwords, realize I'm giving myself a headache, then say, "It's too early, I'm still talking to people, Art. Before we knew that there was city money going into the project, we had concerns about the size. Now," I take a breath, "I'm not sure. If I need any more information, I'll call you."

He may have been about to grovel but I've hung up. It bothers me to see such an obvious sucking-up stance.

Besides, I have company.

Clarice is hanging at my door, making not-so-subtle "psssstt" noises at a volume that has newsroom heads turning.

"Yes, Clar, I'm yours now. What's up?"

"Not a whole lot. Oh, Suzy managed to get some assisted housing through Victim Witness. She'll move tomorrow. And, oh, they arrested Gunther."

"What?" I know my shout carries across the room as I slam my chair back, run around the desk, haul Clarice into my office and shut the door so fast it vibrates. This isn't any news the other reporters and editors won't learn, but I want to make sure we have the story framed and ready before any rumor mills start grinding out.

"So, when did this happen?"

She rubs her arm where I tugged her. "Geez, Amy, I told you Suzy would probably be discharged today or tomorrow."

"Are you trying to give me an ulcer, Clar? Not Suzy, Gunther."

"Oh, that. The BOLO worked. They spotted his truck near Tracy. He wasn't fleeing, just visiting some old friends. Hadn't even realized they were looking for him and lost it when three cop cars pulled up at his pal's house. He was seriously pissed off and resisted arrest."

"What are the charges, besides resisting arrest?"

"Growing illegal substances with the intent to sell, aggravated assault with a lethal weapon, fleeing the scene of a crime."

CHAPTER TWENTY-SIX

"Leaving the scene of a crime? What crime?"

If Clarice continues to roll her eyes like that, she'll give herself a headache. Or they'll get stuck. "The crime scene at Suzy's, well his, house."

Now I'm eye-rolling. "Wait a minute. He pulls an aggravated assault then the cops expect him to stick around?"

"No, no...he ran over the neighbor's mailbox on his way out. The cops are calling it a hit and run. Just a good way to add to the charges."

"I'd have thought there was enough without that."

She's waving her notebook in front of her face, fanning it to catch a breeze even though the air conditioning keeps the building cool. Then I look closely and realize she came from the sheriff's office in a hurry.

"What's wrong? Why are you so out of breath?"

"I tried to call you a buncha times on my way over, but it always went directly to voicemail." She shrugs. "So, I ran. The heat's a bitch."

My mouth drops open. The visual of the disheveled blond running full-tilt down the afternoon street in the ninety-eight degree heat stuns me. At least today she's in jeans and a tee. As I'm absorbing this, she pulls her hair back and stuffs it in a ponytail using a rubber band off my desk. I wonder if the newsprint ink on the band will streak her hair.

"Suzy must be happy with this news."

"I don't think she knows yet."

"Didn't anybody tell her?"

"It just happened. They haven't even processed him yet."

"How do you know all this?"

She takes a breath. "Because I was going out the back parking lot when they brought him in. I figured they were headed for an interrogation room so I went around to the front and sauntered in like I do every afternoon. People were in little groups, whispering. I said, 'Hey, what's up?' and they scattered like I'd turned a fire hose on. Gave me a perfect chance to follow DeBennedetti to his desk and ask him."

My head was in my hands. "Clarice, one of these days this is going to come back to bite us."

"What? I didn't do anything out of the ordinary."

"That may be, Clar. And that might be the problem. You're comfortable over there, the Sheriff trusts you and you're friends with a lot of the deputies. It's a different game now. The state guys have come into this high profile case and they're not as friendly or as casual. Not what you're used to."

I sense her hackles beginning to rise. "Neither Krutz or Wilkes were there..."

"Whether or not they're in the building doesn't matter. It's that they have a presence now. The whole office is probably walking on eggs waiting for some comment or crossing of some line to work its way up to Sacramento. You know as well as I do that there's always jockeying for position over there. They talk a team game—and certainly put up a blue wall when there's any criticism. They're just like a family, bicker among themselves until an outsider appears, then it's all together, happily ever after."

"You may be right, Amy, but I'm not going to change who I am or how I do things just because of a couple of suits from Sacramento...or wherever. I'll keep a lower profile while they're in town, though."

I give her a small smile, recognition that I understand her concession. "What's next?"

"I'm thinking that with Gunther in jail, Suzy might as well go back to her house, once she can get around."

"The house is still a crime scene. When will it get released?"

Clarice is quiet. I watch the chess game of her thoughts chase across her face, then "They've already processed most of it. Blood samples, fingerprints, photos. Gunther just threw the baseball bat into the garden when he stormed off. It took 'em an hour or so to find it...as they were chopping down the corn and marijuana. They'll probably release it in a couple of days."

"OK, I'm giving you a chore that you may not like."

She raises her hand to wave me away, then stops. "What?" There's all the suspicion of being conned.

"You need to go over and talk to Krutz and 'Just call me Harry'..." I've lost her.

"Who's 'Just call me Harry'?"

"Sorry, that's what he said to me when we were introduced. Harrison Wilkes. He's the better of the two. Anyway, you need to know what's going on with the drug investigation. Are they trying to tie Gunther into the corporation yard killings?"

"Huh. Like they'd tell me that!" She snorts.

"You're a great reporter, Clar. You can use finesse, I've seen it. I know you don't like dealing with the stuffed shirts and by-the-book guys, but you can when the payoff is information."

She stands up and gathers her stuff—notebook, paperclips, pens and all—gives a huff of agreement? disagreement? pique?, pulls the door open and steers for her desk. I've told her the truth, she can be tactful when it's needed. It takes more energy than she's usually willing to give. She must have watched too many reruns of Dragnet when she was a kid, she's the "just the facts, ma'am" news gatherer, but she'll find the story any way she can.

I busy myself with a few more irate phones calls about the Harvest of Praise, traffic, and taxpayer bills as I watch the clock. I can barely hear Gwen's voice as she talks to the gadfly who's appointed himself the guardian of the public good where the city's concerned. He was the one who called with the tip to look at the city budget carefully. His conversations usually edge along the thin line between conspiracy and reason, but this time he's hit a home run. There'll be no ignoring him, now.

The tenor of Gwen's voice is changing. It sounds as though she's wrapping it up in a friendly manner so I send her a quick note to see me. She stands up, waves at me, points to the bathroom and disappears. In a few minutes, she's at my office door.

"How are you holding up?"

"I'm OK, Amy. It's going to take more time than I thought, unraveling all the threads in this. Kenny is trying to find a way to turn this into a criminal suit, but I don't think that's going to fly."

"A criminal suit? Is he alleging that the church deliberately set out to bilk the city? He's believing too much of his own realities."

"I know. The worst of this is that now he'll see collusion in every decision the city makes. And he'll call me." Gwen's mouth turns into a grimace and she rubs her eyes. "I didn't sign up for this kind of grief."

She's right. I tell her my story of covering city hall after Vinnie wanted me to find something safe. I was interviewing the mayor for a personality feature when a disgruntled city worker came bursting in, waving a gun. I ducked under the desk, the SWAT negotiators showed up, everybody finally calmed down with no shots fired, I had a page one story and Vinnie and I didn't speak for two days.

We never know what's going to be in store when we get out of bed in the morning.

CHAPTER TWENTY-SEVEN

Clarice strolls back in from the sheriff's office, subdued from her mad dash earlier. I hope Krutz and Wilkins haven't chewed her out. She glances up at my windows and I wave her in.

"Anything new? You look like you've been verbally bashed."

"No, not really. I do hate talking to those straight-laced guys. Every other sentence was 'This is an on-going investigation. We have no comment.' When are they going to comment? After everything's been wrapped up and there's no interest any more?"

I suspect that the cops would be happier if they could just do their jobs with no media attention, but at least we've come a long way since the days of the Hearst-Pulitzer circulation wars.

During the summer of 1897, New York was riveted with the news of a murder, complete with missing body parts and a torso found in a ditch by two boys. Hearst hired a bunch of young reporters, issued them bicycles and dubbed them the "Murder Squad." They spent their time interviewing witnesses, chasing down leads and interfering with the investigation. Their hunt culminated on June 30, 1897 when Hearst's Journal ran a page one story, "Solved by the Journal; Mrs. Nack, Murderess."

Yellow journalism is pretty much dead in the mainstream press. I'm happy—most of the time. Occasionally, I'd love to be able to say we helped solve something, but there's still the rush of uncovering mischief, mayhem, malfeasance and just plain wrong-doing.

"Maybe they won't comment on some things. There's still enough here. Gunther's arrested and being questioned, the cops—probably DEA—have torn out his crop. Suzy's garden is trampled. Write this up for page one tomorrow. If you'd like, I'll authorize some overtime and you can go talk to the neighbors this weekend. They've got to be spinning, seeing Gunther get his."

She nods her head. It frosts her that Krutz is playing so tight, but overtime is a tasty carrot. I know how much, or how little, Clarice makes and a few extra bucks are welcome.

It's time to put on my real mom hat. Heather should be rolling in from Santa Barbara any time now, and I want to be home to greet her. Walking to my car, the heat feels palpable, heavy, weighing everything down. At home, even the summer flowers, so jaunty when I left this morning, are limp, gasping for air and water.

"I'll give you guys a drink when the sun's set," I tell them. I've learned not to water during the day, it just evaporates.

Mac is sprawled on the cool entry tile. He manages to give a few tail thumps and I finally coax him out to the back for a potty break. I reset the air to seventy degrees, cooler than I normally have it for me. Heather's been living on the coast and, even though it's Southern California, the Pacific still sends breezes. She'll have to get acclimated to the valley heat again when she moves back in a month or so.

I'm pulling a tee over my head when I hear the front door slam.

"Hey, Mac, how's the boy!" I picture Heather dropping her bags on the floor and plopping down to give Mac a short roughhouse and a big ear rub. I'm right. When I walk in, they're both on the floor, Mac squirming and Heather giggling. There's a prickle behind my eyes, but I don't let on. Heather hates it when I get maudlin.

She scrambles to her feet and gives me a hug and a peck on the cheek. I console myself that I'd probably strain something if I tried to do a Mac greeting.

"Hi sweetie, how was the drive?" She's packed a duffle as well as her backpack which feels heavy for a casual weekend. "You bringing rocks for Mac or something?"

"Funny. No, I'm studying for the national boards. I have to take them right after I graduate."

"Are you really planning to study this weekend?" I roll my eyes as I turn my back and start up the stairs to her room. This is the young woman who'd party hardy the night before finals. She'd manage to scrape through every time. Studying is just one more sign that she's turned the corner to grown-up-hood.

After she's settled, I pull out the wine and cheeses, add some grapes and take the food back to the patio. It's a tad cooler by the pool and I'm happy to have her here. I've gotten used to her being gone and don't get so despondent any more when she leaves to take up her real life again.

"What's your schedule like for this weekend?"

She takes a sip of wine. "I have six or seven places I want to look at tomorrow, then tomorrow night some of us from high school are getting together for drinks and dinner. Sunday, I was hoping you could quiz me on some of the practice tests for the nationals."

Sounds packed to me, but I'm usually leading a quiet existence. "Do you want me to go to Sacramento with you?"

"I don't want to take up your whole weekend with my stuff, but, sure, I'd like that."

She may be grown-up. I'd still walk across hot coals for her. "Sure, I'll go. I don't have much to do. Where are you looking?"

As I heat the barbecue to cook some skewered chicken, Heather pulls a sheaf of print-outs from her search. "I'm kind of torn. A few of these are small houses in the area of the hospital. I'd love a house. I could get a dog. I'm not so sure that I want to take care of a yard, though. There's a lot more maintenance with a house.

"I'm also interested in the mid-town area. It's gotten funky and interesting. Lots of coffee houses, small restaurants, shops, people on the streets. It's more of a neighborhood than I remember."

I pull together a Greek salad and take that, plates, silverware out to the table. "Either of those areas would be a good choice. It's much quieter around the hospital, settled and residential. Mid-town apartments, you'll meet more people your age."

Heather nods as we begin to eat. "I'm going to keep an open mind. Someplace is going to have my name on it."

****

By Sunday night, she's run through her agenda. She's signed a lease on a small, two-bedroom house five blocks from the hospital. It has a garage in the back, a covered patio, an orange tree and room for a dog. I've gone through the test questions with her, she had dinner with friends, she's even spent a couple of hours by the pool with two (male) high school buds. She'll leave before I get up in the morning. We spend some time going over the logistics of her move, I offer again to drive down and help, she says no thanks, again, and we hug each other good-bye.

When I see her again in a few weeks, she'll be a well-launched young woman with amazing pleasures and challenges ahead of her.

It's bittersweet.

I need to talk to someone. I call Nancy, but her phone goes to voicemail.

Phil answers on the second ring. "Everything alright? Your voice sounds funny."

I take a breath. I don't want to come across as too needy, probably the fastest way to chase a guy off. "I'm fine, just a little overwhelmed. Heather's been here this weekend."

"Didn't it go well? Did you have a fight?"

"No, and that's the problem. It was wonderful. She showed up with an agenda, got everything accomplished and is heading back to Santa Barbara for her last final and to take the national boards. She even found a house."

I can almost see the laugh wrinkles as Phil says, "Gee, I'm sorry you enjoyed a weekend with your daughter. I should take notes so we can have the same."

"Gaacckkk. That's not the point. It's sinking in that my daughter is a grown-up. I'm feeling a little redundant."

Now the laugh is there. His voice deepens as he says, "Redundant? I don't think you can even claim that word. Heather may be moving away from needing you. I'm not, though."

CHAPTER TWENTY-EIGHT

When I hang up, I'm smiling. A spot of warmth sits in my chest as I get ready for bed but worry drifts in as I try to fall asleep. What does that mean? Does Phil want to keep me around? Is this for the long-term, or is he saying that he's having fun, wanting to stay light?

Or is he wanting me to take the responsibility for the next step?

I finally fall into a deep sleep and don't hear Heather leave. What I do hear, and feel, is Mac pacing at the side of my bed. He'd slept with Heather and she must have let him out. Now, she was gone, he was hungry and I was somewhat available.

It was only seven, earlier than my usual eight-thirty. Once awake, I wasn't going back to sleep. "C'mon, little guy, I'll give you some crunchies."

Fortified with a big mug of French Roast, I logged on to see if I'd missed anything.

I had the usual note from the night copy editor, listing the times that pages got out to the backshop and to the pressroom. Everything went smoothly and no overtime for any of the union people. This wasn't in my job description, but if I kept a tab on all the expenses and overtime, I had armor if the publishers asked questions.

A note from Clarice, who'd spent part of the weekend in the Delta, talking to folks. "Went well, found some women. Let's talk in the morning."

Hmmm, cryptic. I couldn't call her now, she'd be asleep, so it had to wait until eleven when she blew in to the office.

And one from Phil that came in just after midnight. I was skittery. Why did he email me after we talked? Was he sorry he'd exposed some need for me?

I take a big swallow of coffee, close my eyes and hit it open.

"Not sleeping well, thinking of you, can't wait for the weekend, love, Phil."

Wow, that isn't a four-letter word I expected and I inhale the mouthful of coffee—and make it to the sink before I choke. After spitting most of it down the drain, I manage to stop coughing, take a deep breath and go back to my laptop.

Calmer, I reread the brief message. Had he spent a tossing-turning night as I had? *Don't analyze everything, just say you're looking forward to it.* I typed "Looking forward" and hit send before I can pick it apart any further.

A ping and "Good, we'll talk later" pops up.

As long as I'm up and restless, I snap a leash on Mac and we burst out into the warm morning. It will be hot this afternoon and evening; now was the best time for our long walk. I steer us by the demolished house, wondering if they'd begun rebuilding. They'd finished demolition, moved in a bulldozer and were scraping soil and dumping it into hazardous waste containers.

So, OK, the absentee landlord rented it out to meth cookers. Chances are he'd plead ignorance and leave the tenants hanging. All of them should be arrested. I'm not a puritan about some drugs. I think weed should be legalized. The reason most drugs are dangerous is that they're controlled substances and therefore open to huge profits for selling and distributing.

Meth, though, uses dangerous chemicals that pollute the air, the ground, the neighborhood and are likely to explode.

Home, I pour another cup of coffee, skim the Sacramento and San Francisco papers, shower, pull on a cotton skirt and a tee, do a minimum make-up, slide on a pair of sandals and head in to work. It'll be at least two hours before Clarice comes in and I can use the time to assign other stories and meet with Gwen.

When I've had a few minutes to read over the local budget of stories to see what the reporters are working on, I spot Gwen coming in. I'm glad that I have some extra time this morning, she looks as though she's had a night like mine. Though I'm sure her's didn't come from stewing over another man while lying next to her best friend/husband.

I wave her into my office and see she has circles under her eyes that make-up isn't covering. "What's up?" Not an original line, but enough so she heaves a sigh that starts at her knees.

"I had a note on my windshield this morning."

"A threat?" I reach for the phone to all the city cops.

"No, no, not a threat, exactly."

"Well, what, exactly?"

She hands me a piece of paper that she's stuffed in her pocket. It's crumpled. I take it. It's plain printer paper, the kind that sells by the ream at any office supply or discount store. As I smooth it out, I realize the note was written on a computer. Fat chance that anything about this can be traced.

It has some Biblical quotes from Revelations that I don't recognize, then says, "Are you part of the beast? Stop telling lies about our church and listening to those who would oppose us! This is a warning from your neighbors."

The hate oozing from this single piece of paper stuns me. "Oh, Gwen, I'm so sorry. Do some of your neighbors belong to the church?"

"I don't really know. It's not a close neighborhood, we nod and say hello when we're out in the yard, but I'm not real friends with any of them."

"Do you have any idea who left this?"

She shakes her head, looking down at the note. "No clue. It's so anonymous. That's why it shakes me up. If I knew who did it, I'd maybe understand. But this, just a random person who hates me?" She shivers.

"Do you want me to pull you off the story?" I don't do this often, taking a reporter off a story that he or she has invested time in, but even though Gwen isn't seeing this as a threat, it still makes me nervous.

"No, I don't want to be pulled. This is an important story and needs to be told. I'm ticked that the church leaders managed to pull the Chamber of Commerce in and then put together a plan that uses city money for their own purposes. That's cheating and lying and it makes me mad."

I understand her. If anyone called her an investigative reporter she'd probably deny it, but this chicanery needs to be exposed.

"Well, what do you want to do?" Unless it leads her into danger, Gwen can handle it any way she's comfortable. "They must know you. They certainly know where you live."

"It makes me slightly nervous, but I've never hidden where I work or what I do. I may not know who this is, but they know me. Whether I stay on this story or not, they can find me. I won't run chicken from people who want to hide behind a church."

I know Gwen is a good, conscientious, reliable reporter, but now I'm feeling as though I haven't given her the credit and backing she deserves.

"Gwen, it's your decision. I have to say that I'm extremely proud of you for taking this stance. If at any time you feel uncomfortable, let me know and we'll rearrange coverage. And please keep me in the loop."

Then a thought occurs to me. "Does your husband know about the note?"

"No." She shakes her head so hard I'm thinking whiplash. "No, and please don't tell him. He wouldn't understand."

She's right.

CHAPTER TWENTY-NINE

Clarice has come in while I'm talking to Gwen and waits, as patiently as she ever waits. Meaning she only waves at me three or four times, just making sure I've seen her.

She steps back as Gwen leaves my office. Maybe she noticed her co-worker is more quiet than usual, so she says, "What's up with Gwen?" I give her two stars for noticing and deduct three for her abrupt comment.

"She had a nasty note on her car this morning."

"A threat? Did you call the cops? I haven't gone over yet, should I check on it?"

"Don't make a big deal about it, Clar. Gwen is ignoring it for now. It's not a threat, just a hate note."

The blond sits down heavily, almost overbalancing and pushing the chair sideways. She grabs the side of my desk to steady her and pulls herself around to face me.

"That kind of cowardice makes me sick. Was it about the church? What a bunch of hypocrites. They talk about kindness and charity then leave anonymous notes taking aim at the messenger."

It's true, leaving anonymous notes is the coward's way. Clarice has been on the receiving end of it, as have I, and it's scary and slimy and personal and underhanded and...

"So, that's Gwen. Now what's going on in the Delta.?" I watch Clarice speed-shift gears like a drag race.

"I talked to a bunch of Suzy's friends. Everybody's glad that Gunther's in the slammer and quite a few of them would like to see him stay there for a good, long time. He's not at the top of anyone's favorite list and most of the time he doesn't make the top one hundred."

"What's the biggest gripe they have against him?" I'm making circles around boxes on a note pad and wonder if there's some deep need to add bars.

"It's a long list." Clarice flips open a new notebook that hasn't had time to collect the usual detritus. "The women are livid at the way he's treated Suzy. They've seen this going on over the last four or five years and watched it get worse. The consensus is they hope he 'hangs by his balls'."

"That's going to keep them out of the jury pool."

She grins.

"What else? Any comments about his growing?"

Her eyes drift beyond me and I know she's pulling up images of the guys she talked to. "A lot of the men are as angry as the women. Not because of Suzy, I don't think. Gunter's actions have brought way too much scrutiny from the law. Nobody came right out and said that they're growing too, but a few of them looked shifty when I asked about the cultivation charges."

"Do you know if Krutz and his merry men have search warrants on any of the other properties?"

Clarice shakes her head. "I haven't asked, they haven't said, but I think not yet. The problem is that all the guys are scared of raids so I'd bet they've pulled their crops. Because of Gunther and his violent temper, they've lost at least a year's worth of profits."

I'm quiet now. The economy of much of the Delta is precarious. Outside of the large agribusinesses that own whole islands, small farmers struggle with market crops, small marinas get by on boat slip rentals and everybody relies on tourist traffic during the summer. Because the alluvial soil is so rich, it has to be tempting to put in a few plants for quick cash.

"He's also had run-ins with a few of his near neighbors." Clarice is flipping notebook pages. "I told you about the gun and little girl incident, didn't I? A lot of the men think he's wound too tight. They stay clear. One said, 'Being around him, it's like waiting for a bomb to go off. You know it's there but you don't know when the timer's set for'."

"Good quote, Clar." Now I'm doodling what could be small explosions. I look up at her. "Did you get the feeling that there's any Posse movement out there?"

Her brows furrow. "No, I don't think so. They're so secretive, I'm not sure I'd notice." She shakes her head. "Oh, I'd probably notice. Anyone spouting anti-government slogans, walking around carrying guns. For sure not wanting to talk to me. No, these people are just average Joes, wanting to live a quiet life, maybe make a few bucks growing, stay out of sight of the cops."

Her version sounds bucolic and rural, a little slice of what a peaceful life was like before the modern age. Drowsy afternoons in summer, the slam of a screen door, the sound of a baseball bat hitting something. Problem was, the baseball bat was hitting Suzy and the screen door slammed because the neighbor was running and screaming for the cops.

"There's also the jealousy."

"What jealousy? Who's jealous of whom?"

She looks at me. "Gunther was on permanent disability. Some of the neighbors were jealous that he sat in his backyard a lot of days, just drinking beer and watching his garden grow."

"Hmmm...that's the disability that caused him to lose his truck, right?"

"Right. Suzy thinks that's what made him so violent. He'd never hit her before that."

"What happened?"

"Suzy said he was in an accident. The truck wasn't badly damaged but Gunther's back went out and he never recovered. Once he wasn't traveling all the time, his anger just grew and..." Her eyes light up. "Traveling. He was traveling after they moved to the Delta. What was he hauling?"

"I don't know, isn't that easy enough to find out? There must be manifests, records somewhere."

"I'll check at the sheriff's office. I'm sure they don't track truck movements, but the CHP? The DMV?"

"Try the Public Utilities Commission, the feds, customs. Even as an independent, he must have filed something with somebody." The hunt may have gotten to me. So what if he went from Point A to Point B by way of Point C? Maybe, though, if we track his movements, we might see a pattern.

"Sure." Clarice has found a spoor now. "What's to say that he didn't pick up a load, swing by the Delta and pick up some unregistered load, drive to a spot where he dropped the unregistered stuff and boogied to his legitimate destination?"

This is a pretty thin supposition, but it would fit with the fact that Gunther became a different person when he wasn't able to drive any more.

"Do you think that he may have had something to do with the murders in the corp yard next to his house?" I'm knitting with conspiracy yarn now.

Clarice drums her pen on the desk to a song in her head, then looks up at me. "I don't know about that. You think the murdered guys saw something that Gunther was doing? Maybe they saw his plants? Maybe they saw him loading his pickup or his truck?"

"I don't know. I don't want to throw the book at the guy, but so much is suddenly revolving around Gunther."

"As you always say, Amy, everything's worth a question." She nods at me as she heads for the sheriff's office.

What have I done, letting her loose with a half-baked theory?

CHAPTER THIRTY

This is starting to make a map in my head. I always wonder when a bunch of seemingly unrelated facts spring up then all begin pointing in one direction.

An examination of state government's plan to help solve California's incessant water woes by building tunnels under the Delta has morphed into a swirling mess of violence, drugs and murder.

I haven't heard much from the Stop the Tunnels crowd and think it's time for another visit to the neighborhood.

Once I'm on my way with the top down on my Miata I'm curious why I don't do this more often. Just thirty miles away from the valley, the Delta is kept cooler, moister, by the Sacramento River. And air from the Pacific and San Francisco Bay funnels up the river's path, with a breeze.

Probably some strange guilt that I shouldn't be out playing hooky on a work day. I should be sitting in the office, glued to my computer screen.

Oh, well.

I find two well-maintained homes in Walnut Grove with Stop the Tunnels signs in the front yard and talk to a woman and a man, asking how their opposition is going.

The woman, Judith Flesser, sighs. "It's an uphill battle. This is such a huge state and there are so many people who don't even know where their water comes from. If you say 'Delta' to them, most of 'em would think you mean the Mississippi Delta. I'm not holding out much hope for stopping the tunnels."

She's probably right. Even though eight million or more people live in the Bay Area and this part of northern California, more than twenty million live in Southern California. And those are the people who will vote for the money to build the tunnels.

Johnny Killops, Judith's next door neighbor is more determined. "We'll stop them. We stopped the Peripheral Canal thirty years ago and we'll stop the tunnels, too."

"How do you plan to do that?" I admire his spunk, wonder about his abilities.

"It's mostly education. We're planning a big media campaign in Southern California. We're raising money for it now."

I've heard some noise about raising money, but I didn't think it was for media buys. "What about the suit? There's been some talk of one."

Killops shrugs. "Yeah, we've talked to one of those public interest law firms in the city but we don't have enough money for a retainer yet. We're hoping one of them will take it pro bono."

As involved in public interest as some of the big firms are, taking a case pro bono that means suing the state, and one that can drag on for years, isn't going to pencil out for the firm's bottom line. The tunnels crowd will be lucky to get the legal research and a filing. These conversations have helped make up my mind about the editorial.

The Monroe *Press* will be against the tunnel proposal. It's a hard decision to make, but there just doesn't seem to be an up side for our area. Having lived in Southern California, I'm aware of the need for more and better water resources, but the tunnels are not the way to go.

As long as I'm out here, I'll drop by Freeland and see what's new at the corporation yard.

There's a truck being loaded with a big drill. No matter what the *Press* says in an editorial, core drilling is going to continue until the state pulls the plug on the contract. I carefully park my car on the street and walk inside the fencing. I don't want any ricocheting equipment swinging around like Clarice ran into.

I wave at a guy who's guiding the drill. He nods and mouths "Just a minute." When the drill's on the truck, he comes over.

"You really can't be in the yard, Miss. It's too dangerous and our insurance carrier would have a fit."

"I know, I don't want to hold anything up." I introduce myself and the man's expression freezes.

"Are you here because that other gal from the paper got hurt? I'll have to call our project manager. I'm not allowed to talk to anyone about it." He's walking off and pulling his cell out of his pocket.

"No, no, I was just curious about the thefts. You installed surveillance cameras. Has it helped?"

He slows and turns to me. "Why are you asking?"

I sense a flash of suspicion from him. He's just a worker—isn't he?

"I get press releases every so often from the Contractor's Board with lists of thefts from construction sites. Equipment, supplies, metals now that the metals market is so strong. I haven't heard about this site since the two guys were killed." A thought. "Did you know them?"

He stiffens and his eyes go flat. "Yeah, I knew them."

"Were you friends? Have they been replaced?"

"Naw, we weren't really friends. Just guys you work with, you know? There are a couple of different companies with contracts out here. I only knew them from here. There's one new guy, haven't worked with him before Again, why are you asking?"

I look around. I'm in a big area full of heavy equipment, surrounded by cyclone fencing and no people visible in the afternoon heat. The worker is burly and leans down to pick up a tool, a big wrench? Have I done what I nag Clarice about, gone off and told nobody where I am or when I'll be back?

"No reason." I'm backing up toward the street entrance, wondering if I left my phone in the car. If I reach in my purse to check will it spook him? "I was wondering if it was hard to work at a place where people were killed."

He takes a step toward me. "It's kinda spooky, but a job's a job. This is a state contract so it pays good." Then he shakes his head and raises the hand with the tool in it. "One bad thing is that some of these guys haven't been on a crew together before. They leave tools lying around. Not smart."

Not smart? I remember that the cops never found the heavy, blunt object used to kill the two workers. Am I looking at a murder weapon?

"I'm not officially the foreman, but I tell these guys to put stuff away." He keeps walking toward me, I keep backing up then realize he's headed to a pickup with a big tool chest mounted on the side. He drops the wrench in, snaps the lid shut. "Any more questions, I gotta call the manager. You really shouldn't be here."

I agree with him. "I'll leave now, thanks for talking to me. I hope the cops find whoever murdered those other guys." If I edge to the side, I can get out of the yard without turning my back on him. I'm digging my keys out of my purse and find my phone as he gets into the big truck and pulls out, waving at me.

Have I scared myself? Maybe I lost my nerve and imagine killers loose everywhere. I remember that Clarice talked to Mark Cruz who lives near here and was one of Gunther's neighbors.

Easier talking to him. I doubt he has a big wrench.

CHAPTER THIRTY-ONE

Mark Cruz isn't too hard to find. He's in his front yard, digging a post hole for a new mailbox.

If his is the mailbox Gunther ripped out, he'll be talkative. I introduce myself and tell him I have his name from Clarice, who was out here a week or so ago.

"I remember her. Blond gal. Almost got run over by one of these idiots." He waves his hand at the cyclone fencing. "I watched 'em put in the surveillance cameras. Don't know if they've seen anything. It's a shame about those two drivers who got killed."

"Are you against the tunnels?" Might as well find out which side Cruz falls on.

"Yeah, I guess so. I'm not a farmer but a lot of them out here are pretty steamed. I just think it's a big waste of money. Plus, this whole Delta is so fragile, it's all silt, you know. Washed down from the mountains over a million or so years ago."

"Are you a geologist?" I eye him. He's wearing the typical retirement uniform, jeans and a plaid shirt over a white tee.

"No. Drove heavy equipment, those big earthmovers and dozers. Worked on a lot of CalTrans jobs. That's kinda why I watch the yard there."

He's a retired guy who watches the corporate yard? Have the cops talked to him yet?

When I ask him this, he leans on his shovel and stares at me. "About what?"

"Well, anything? Did they ask if you saw something when the drivers' bodies turned up?"

"They did, for all the good it did."

"Why?"

"I wasn't home."

The men were killed in the early evening hours. If Cruz is retired, where was he during these hours? "Were you working?"

"Naw, I wasn't here. I took some time and went fly-fishing in the Eastern Sierra. You ever go there?"

I close my eyes as the memories wash over me. Vinnie and I drove up highway 395 on a short vacation one year, ending up at Mammoth Mountain, skiing. Neither of us were any good, but we loved playing in the snow, so rare for Southern California people like us. It was a magic time and I'm pretty sure that's when I got pregnant with Heather.

I look at Cruz. "Yep, once when I lived in the LA area. It's different from this side of the Sierra."

"It is. There's a beauty all its own though. I try and get to June Lake every year. Anyway, that's where I was when those guys were murdered. I probably didn't spend more than an hour talking to the cops."

"You and Clarice talked a bit about Gunther Mohre, right?"

"We did." Cruz stabs the shovel in the dirt hard enough that it stands up. "He's just not a nice guy."

"Did you ever have words with him?"

"Not really. I stayed as clear as I could from him. Watched him get into shouting matches with some of the other neighbors, though."

"What was he upset about? Think he took your mailbox out deliberately?"

Cruz rubs his chin. "No, I don't imagine he even knew he'd hit the box. He was tearing outta here too fast to pay any attention. That was usual for him. He'd convince himself that one of the other neighbors was spying on him, checking out his backyard, nosing into his 'business', whatever that was."

There's a tick of silence then, "Guess I know what some of his business was after all. The cops were over there. Lots of yellow crime scene tape and a crew with shovels and machetes. Harvesting." He smiles, happy with himself for being flip.

"I guess you heard that he's been caught?"

He nods. "Think the charges will stick this time?"

Now it's my turn to nod. "I think so. His arraignment is today. Clarice is covering it. We've heard rumors that the DA is going for no-bail."

"Pffftt...even if there's bail set, Gunther's not gonna get bailed out. He has this property, sure, but Suzy's the only family he has and she's sure not going to go to any trouble for him. Not this time."

It's been quiet in the hot summer air as we've been talking. Now a car comes slowly down the street, as though the driver's looking for a house number. Cruz follows with his eyes and I wonder if he's memorizing the license plate.

Sensing I'm watching, he glances back to me and grimaces. "We just have so little traffic on this street. I pretty much know everybody who drives by. Except for that SUV."

I look at the street. It's a longish block that dead-ends on the other side of the corporate yard. There are half-a-dozen houses on this side of the street, then Cruz' then Gunther's. We're two blocks off the main levee road and the whole neighborhood isn't more than maybe twenty homes. I can understand how Cruz knows everybody, but I don't see an SUV.

"What SUV? I don't see one."

"It's gone. It was parked here on and off for days. It must have showed up when I was fishing and stayed until Gunther took off."

"Did you ever see anyone in it? Or get out of it?" Sounds like someone has had surveillance on this area. Who? The feds? Surely they would have let the local sheriff know... or maybe not.

One of the Posse members? No, they wouldn't be so obvious. They'd put on camo, paint their faces and sneak in the backyards at night.

Maybe someone from the drug distribution group. Had Gunther shorted somebody on one of his deliveries?

"Do you think that the yard's cameras might have caught it on their video?" If the SUV was there for several days, it should stick out.

"It won't be on those videos, the cameras are all pointing at the yard. It might be on mine, though."

His?

He has surveillance video cameras? Mark Cruz has sounded like a sane reasonable man during our chat. Is he a fringe groupie?

"You have surveillance cameras?" If I ask why, will he think I'm prying? "How long have you had them?"

"Not long. I got them last year before I went fishing. I'd had some vandalism when I was gone and I just wanted to catch them."

Is he some sort of vigilante, doing his own version of justice? "What kind of vandalism? Did you report it to the sheriff?"

"No, I didn't bother. It was just some plants pulled up..." he catches sight of my shocked expression. "Not that kind of plant, some impatiens and pansies...just summer color annuals. I know it was neighborhood kids. I wanted to get them on video, identify them and show the video to their folks. Kind of shaming them. I hoped it would make them think before they really got themselves into trouble."

"Have you looked at the video since you've been back?"

Cruz shakes his head. "No. Didn't find any vandalism this time. I made a production out of installing the cameras and just knowing that they're there may be a deterrent."

My fingers are beginning to itch. I want to look at that video.

CHAPTER THIRTY-TWO

I open my mouth, about to ask Mark Cruz if I can see his video when my phone starts "Who Let The Dogs Out".

I don't even get out "Hi" before Clarice is talking. "He's been arraigned, biggest charges are attempted murder and assault with a deadly weapon. Bail is $2 million. He's not going anywhere. Where are you?"

She can do a segue faster than any musician. "I'm out in the Delta. Talked to some Stop the Tunnels folks and now I'm in Freeland with Mark Cruz. Write up the arraignment for tomorrow. Can you get some quotes from the DA? What did he use as arguments?"

"Mostly that Gunther is a flight risk. He's been arrested several times, is unemployed and now facing drug charges. Why are you talking to Mark Cruz?"

"I went to the corporation yard but didn't get much from the only guy there, so since I was in the neighborhood—and Cruz was out putting up a new mailbox—I stopped to talk to him. Did he mention an SUV parked on the street to you?"

Silence. I'm thinking I can hear the tape spinning as she goes over her conversation with Cruz.

"No. We just talked about Gunther. Why?"

I've stepped away from Cruz and I lower my voice. "He says there'd been an SUV parked on the street for days when he came back from a trip. Turns out he has surveillance cameras pointed at the street. I'm going to ask him if I can look at the video."

Clarice sucks in a breath. "Amy, that could be evidence! You always preach at me about getting into the investigation. What are you thinking?"

"Oh, pish, Clarice. This won't be evidence. It's not even surveillance of the corporation yard or Gunther's house, it's the street in front of Cruz' house."

"I don't like it. I think you're pushing the envelop, but I guess you're the boss. Be careful." It's good that cell phones just go to dead air. If she'd been on a handset, I'd be deaf from her slamming the phone down.

Apparently, I've hit a nerve. Is she ticked at me for getting in the middle of her story? Does she think Jim Dodson will be upset? Maybe she's miffed at herself because I've uncovered a piece she hadn't found.

I run a hand through my hair, hitch my purse up on my shoulder, turn to Cruz. "Can we go take a look at your video?"

He seems surprised. "Sure, I guess. I don't think there's anything to see. Let me put these tools away."

Tools. This is my afternoon for interest in tools. Cruz starts up his driveway and motions for me to follow.

"I'll put these in the shed. We can go in through the kitchen." He's carrying a posthole digger and a shovel, both of which look heavy.

At least I've talked to Clarice. She knows where I am, who I'm with and what I'm doing—even though she may not approve. If I don't show up or check in with her in thirty minutes or so, she'll be on the phone again. I'm not getting any creepy vibes from Mark Cruz, but feel much safer following him into his house when I know someone has my back.

I wait on a small patio while Cruz stows the tools in the shed. He comes over, opens the door into the kitchen and we go in. It's cooler and darker inside, out of the glare of the sun.

"Would you like something to drink? I have soda, iced tea, water?"

"No thanks." I'm leery of taking anything from a source. I don't want him thinking we have some sort of bargain. "You know I'm not working on a story now. This is just for background."

He glances up as he's getting his laptop ready on a kitchen table. "All off the record?" He has a slight smile. "I always wanted to say that."

"Right." To show good faith, I put my purse with notepad and pens on a chair, after I pull my phone out and slip it in my skirt pocket.

"OK, here we go." He hits a few keys and the view of his street pops up on the screen.

"What are we looking at?" I'm squinting to focus, he didn't buy the top of the line in cameras.

"The street." There's a condescension in his voice.

"I'm sorry, I wasn't clear. When was this?"

He hits another key and the time-date stamp appears. "This was about a month ago."

"Can we look at the video from the time you were gone?"

"Sure. I was going to edit most of it but haven't gotten around to it. Here it is."

It's still the street in front of his house. A pickup goes into the corporation yard, then one of the big trucks carrying the drill comes out. Two kids come out of the house across the street with a baseball, mitt and bat and head out of the frame. A car heads down the street and pulls into a driveway.

Then, there it is. A light-color SUV, an import, cruises down the street and parks across from Cruz'. Nobody gets out. The back windows are tinted so dark not even a shadow is visible.

After three hours, Gunther backs his pickup out of his driveway, missing Cruz' mailbox, and burns rubber, heading out. The driver of the SUV waits for a few minutes, flips a u-turn and sedately leaves.

Well, this is riveting.

I sit through another two days of video, fast-forwarding and skipping all nighttime activity, and the pattern stays the same. The SUV shows up mid-morning, parking in front of different houses and moving around during the day. As soon as Gunther leaves, the SUV waits for a few minutes and follows him.

By now, I can tell it's a newish Toyota and see the plate number as it makes the u-turn in front of the corporation yard. It's registered in California, like some twenty million or so other cars.

"And that's it?" I look at Cruz who looks back.

"I told you the cameras just cover the street and I didn't have any vandalism during my last fishing trip. This video is about the time of the murders. I haven't bothered to tell the cops about it because it doesn't show anything."

He's right. There's something going on and someone's been watching Gunther, but not much on this tape sheds light on the murders or why Gunther snapped and beat Suzy.

"Mark, I've enjoyed talking with you. Thanks for taking the time to show me the surveillance. I don't know if it's worth anything. By the way, Clarice was at the arraignment and Gunther is being held on attempted murder and assault with a deadly weapon. The judge set bail at $2 million."

"Well..., well...as far as Gunther's concerned it might as well be $1 billion. He's not coming home anytime soon."

He snaps his fingers and I watch a small look of happiness flit across his face. "If he's not coming home, I wonder if Suzy will? There are people here who would love to see her back, help her out. If you see her, will you tell her I asked?"

"I will, and I'll pass that along to Clarice. Thanks again."

I head to my car in a state of wonderment. Will Suzy find safety and happiness out of the train wreck her life had become?

CHAPTER THIRTY-THREE

When Clarice's ringtone starts I find a wide spot to pull over.

She's shown admirable restraint. Only called once in the ninety minutes I was watching paint dry, well, watching the video of Mark Cruz' street.

"What's up." I keep an eye on my rear view mirror. A wide spot on this levee road isn't very wide.

"Have you decided to tell the Sheriff about the video?"

"Yes, Clar, I have. I don't know what good it's going to do. I need you to do something for me."

"What?" Suspicion seeps through my phone.

"Will you chat up your friendly clerk at the city cops and run a license for me?"

"Geez, Amy. You're breaking all of your cautionary lessons. Remember the one about not taking advantage of your sources? Sure, I'll ask her. What is it?"

I reel off the SUV's plate number. "When I get back, I'm going to see Dodson and talk about Mark Cruz. Do you want to come?"

"No, I'm on my way to the cops."

Hmmm, she doesn't want to see Jim Dodson? I'll talk to her about this later. For now I need to get back to the office then the Sheriff's office.

The pink blizzard of "Important" notes has tapered off to a flurry. I wave at the copy desk that I'll read the local stories as soon as I get back then do a fast walk to Dodson. I didn't call first, so I'm risking that he'll be busy, but when I check with his assistant, she waves me into his office.

He's shuffling paperwork, reports from the look of them. I send a silent thanks that we're living in a paperless culture—hah! Dodson looks up and I sense he's heard my thought and added an "Amen" of his own.

"Where are the CHP guys?"

A bit abrupt, but I don't want to mention anything about Cruz in front of them. Just yet.

"Howdy, Amy. Are you the room monitor now?"

Boy, I like this man. His wry sense of humor smooths the way over my impatience and he doesn't ruffle easily. If we weren't such close friends, if Phil wasn't back in my life, if Clarice wasn't interested in him, Dodson and I may have tried to make a go of it.

"Sorry, Jim. I ran across something interesting in the Delta and I'd like you to help me work through it without fuss and bother."

"Have you been nosing into our stuff? Does Clarice know?"

"Yes and yes. I didn't start out to nose, I was talking to some people about the tunnels..." I pause. "You know I'm going to write an editorial about the project, right?"

"I assumed so. Which side are you going to come down on?"

"The anti one, for what good it'll do. The *Press* is a tiny voice in the wilderness when you take in the whole state. That's not what I want to talk about. While I was out there, I drove by the corporation yard."

He huffs out an almost-laugh. "Just can't take the girl out of the chase for adrenaline, huh?"

I can feel my face warming. "Fudge, Jim, I have to ask questions. It's what I do."

"I know. So how's our murder scene?"

"It's not the yard that's so interesting, it's one of Gunther's neighbors. Mark Cruz."

Dodson closes his eyes and I watch him riffling through his mind's Rolodex. "Got it. He's the one who had his mailbox torn out when Gunther took off. Is he still pissed?"

"He didn't seem to be, mostly resigned and glad that Gunther's in jail." This isn't the time or place for injecting a tangent about his possible interest in Suzy. "The interesting thing is that he has a surveillance camera."

Now I have his attention. He rocks back in his chair and nails me with a look. "He didn't mention anything like that to my guys who talked to him. Is he trying to hide it?" Dodson is edging toward mad. At me? At Cruz?

"No, he just doesn't think it's of any value to you."

I spend the next few minutes recapping my afternoon and then hand him my peace offering, the SUV license number.

"Are you sure you didn't see anything else?"

"No, he only has one camera and it's pointing out at his front yard and across the street. He wanted to catch the neighbor kids tearing up his plants."

The Sheriff's eyebrows reach for the sky.

"Not those kind of plants, his summer flowers. He grows impatiens every year."

"You know, I'm going to have to get a warrant and take that video. Maybe our lab can pull more information off of it."

I nod. "I'm sorry I did this, Jim. I don't want to jeopardize any evidence or get in the middle of the case. It was such a weird spur of the moment thing that I couldn't resist. Then, after I asked to see it, I got nervous. The guy in the corp yard was creepy and now I'm going into someone's house to look at possible evidence.

"I always worried about Vinnie. I don't know how you guys do that every day, go into situations where it might not be safe. That's adrenaline I don't want."

Dodson smiles. "You know what they say about policing, hours of boredom punctuated by a minute of sheer terror. I'm surprised that more cops don't have ulcers and heart attacks. Thank you for coming clean with me, Amy. I can't pretend I'm happy with your news, I'd have liked it better if you'd told me and *not* watched it, but you can't unwatch it."

I stand up, pick up my purse and turn to the door. I feel deflated, flat, disappointed in myself. They say that confession is good for the soul. Mine leaves me feeling slightly sleazy. I turn back to him. "Are you going to send someone out this afternoon?"

"Now that this cat is out of this bag, I need to do everything by the book. I'll have to get a warrant first, so it may be later tonight or tomorrow morning before we pay a visit. You're not thinking of calling Cruz first, are you?"

Ooof, low blow. I deserve it, though. "No, I've done enough mischief. I'm going to go back to being a quiet little editor."

This gets a true smile from him. "Oh, I doubt that, Amy. Next time you want to play investigator, please call me instead."

"We do investigations all the time, Jim. I can't promise that we'll call you instead. But the next time I'm offered some evidence in one of your ongoing cases, I'll politely decline. How's that?"

He's standing now, preparing to walk me out. "That's fair." He comes around his desk and puts his hand on my arm, a peace offering of his own. We've come to a good place of trust together. As we come out into the hall, I spot Krutz heading our way. I mouth a quick goodbye and make for the exit door at the other end of the hallway.

I'm sorry that Dodson has to work with this guy. He makes my skin draw up, but I don't want to antagonize him or make it any more difficult for Dodson.

Who knows, we may have to work with the CHP ourselves one day.

CHAPTER THIRTY-FOUR

Clarice and Gwen are in my office with the door closed. This can't be good.

As I open the door I hear they're having a heated discussion...all in whispers.

"What's going on?" I step around my desk, pull a drawer out and sling my purse in. Then stop, pull my purse out, grab my phone, toss the purse again and slam the drawer.

When I look up, they both have a startled look. What have I caught them at. "So tell."

There's silence. They glance at each other then give me a sideways look. Clarice clears her throat and Gwen says, "Well...."

"OK, neither of you usually has a problem talking to me, so talk. You first, Clar."

A tide of pink washes over her neck. "I was telling Gwen that she has to file a report on this.

"On this? What is 'this' Gwen?"

"It's alright, Amy. Just another one of those notes."

Clarice explodes. "Gwen, this isn't an anonymous note on your car!"

"Don't make too big a deal of it, Clarice. You just want to get a chance to talk to the cops." Gwen's back is up. I've never seen her stand up to Clarice like this.

"Somebody better tell me what's happening." Whatever "this" is, the two women are behaving oddly.

Now Gwen gives me a sheepish look. "It's just that I got sort of...well, a kind of...a threat."

"What kind of threat, exactly, Gwen?"

She hangs her head. "Somebody burned part of my lawn."

"That's backing into the story like a chicken, Gwen." Clarice slams her hand down on my desk and I get up and close the door. I'm not sure what's gotten the blond so riled up.

"I just didn't want to make a big deal of this, Clarice." Gwen looks close to tears.

"Too late. It's already a big thing." Clarice is steamed.

"Tell. Me. Now!" They jump. I don't usually raise my voice.

Clarice straightens her shoulders and takes a breath. "When I looked through the cops logs, I found a fire call to a yard fire. The address seemed familiar, so I checked the reverse directory and it was at Gwen's house."

"Is everything alright?" Out of the corner of my eye I can see her shrinking, as though she doesn't want to stand out.

"It's fine, Amy. The fire's out and nothing is damaged."

"If that's the case, why are you two arguing?"

Clarice breathes out exasperation. Glad she's not a dragon, the desk would be on fire. "Tell her the rest of it, Gwen. Tell her what it said."

There's silence again, then Gwen whispers, "It said 666."

Oh, holey moley If this isn't a threat, I don't know what is. "What are the cops doing, Clarice?"

She shrugs. "That's what we were, uhhh, 'discussing' when you came in, Amy. Gwen doesn't want to file a report. She thinks it's just minor vandalism."

An anonymous note on a car, an angry letter to the editor calling a reporter stupid, is mindless vandalism. Pouring gasoline on someone's lawn is property damage. And writing messages like "666" and setting it on fire moves this from plain vandalism to a personal attack.

"I'm so sorry Gwen, but I'm siding with Clarice on this. If you don't get over to the cops immediately, I'll call the chief, myself. I can understand why you want to keep this quiet, but you can't."

"But Amy..." Gwen can't keep her voice steady. "I'll lose my sources, I'll lose credibility on the story about city funds. If I report the fire, people are going to assume that if I write a negative story, I'm retaliating"

She's right. This is touchy. I'll probably have to pull her off the story. "I understand, Gwen, and I hate that this happened. You did nothing. Some low-life scum took control of the situation and your career is collateral damage. Let's think this through, after you file the report. Both of you meet me back here when you're finished."

As they head out the door I'm already dialing Art at the Chamber.

"Well, hi, Amy." His oily voice always sets my teeth on edge.

"I wanted to give you a heads-up Art. There's been some property damage and it's looking like a personal attack. The police are taking a report on it right now."

"I appreciate your telling me this, Amy. It's not the kind of publicity we want to have about Monroe. But what does it have to do with the Chamber?"

"The damage was a yard fire at Gwen's house, you know, the reporter covering the city's involvement with the Harvest of Praise?"

"I'm sorry to hear that, but I'll ask again, what does this have to do with the Chamber?" His voice sounds honestly stumped.

"Somebody wrote 666 in gasoline on Gwen's front lawn then set it on fire. A neighbor called the fire department."

Art's gasp echoes. "You're kidding!"

"No, I wish I were. You wouldn't happen to know anything about this, would you?"

"Absolutely not!"

"Good. I'd hate to think that the Chamber was involved in any way with this...even tacitly."

"Amy, we may be in favor of this project, we believe it's a huge boost to the economy, but there's no way we'd countenance any vandalism. We'd be shooting ourselves in the foot! Anybody would. This kind of thing sets a cause so far back it might never recover."

I let a smile form for the first time since I heard about the fire. I pick up a pen and doodle spiky things that might be flames with big fat drops, tears? rain? water from a fire hose? coming down out of the sky.

"I'm glad to hear you feel that way, Art. Because one of Gwen's neighbors reported the fire, it's a matter of public record and we're going to run a story. I can't remember the last time there was anything like this attack in Monroe."

Art's voice is on the edge of screech. "Are you going to make a big deal about this?"

"It is a big deal, Art. Clarice is at the police station now, getting details. I'm having to pull Gwen off most of the story because she's now a victim in a criminal action that may be involved with the project."

"What proof do you have that the fire has anything to do with the project?"

"I'm thinking the police will have ways to find proof. Forensics is so advanced, they can probably tell what brand of gas was used. Although if someone confessed, I imagine they'd stop the investigation."

I can hear Art's breathing getting rapid. "What do you mean, if someone confessed? Do you know who did it?"

"Of course not, Art. I wouldn't second guess the police. But there must be a person or people in town who do know. And when the arsonist is tied to the Harvest of Praise...that's going to give the project such a huge black eye it may never recover. All that time and money down the drain because some fool thought he was being clever. Oops, Clarice is calling on my other line. I need to take it."

As I click off Art is saying something. It may be "Wait..." but I'm not waiting.

The only way to fight fire is with fire.

CHAPTER THIRTY-FIVE

Clarice actually does call a few minutes later, to tell me they've sent an investigator from the arson squad out with the detective, but they're not hopeful of finding a lot.

"They can figure out what kind of gas or accelerant was used. Lucky for the arsonist we're in a drought, the grass is so dry it didn't take much. Also good that the neighbor spotted it right away. It may have caught some bushes and spread."

"How's Gwen holding up?"

Clarice's voice takes on a lighter note. "She's good. I think she's glad she filed a report. And she was looking at me with interest. She doesn't always appreciate what I do."

Clarice is right. She's so up-front and headline hungry that most of the reporters steer clear of her. Getting one of them to work with her on a project takes a lot of cajoling, carrots and implied threats. She's not mean or nasty, she's so focused on what she needs to find out that she can be oblivious to anyone else's efforts.

"Are you coming back? I just talked with Art at the Chamber of Commerce and wanted to fill you two in on our conversation."

"Leaving now," then dead air.

The two women who show up at my office have a lot better body language than the ones who left a bit ago.

"You're going to have to talk to your husband, you know, Gwen."

She has a wan smile but nods her head. "I know. I'm glad he's been out of town for all of this. He's coming home tomorrow."

I turn to Clarice. "The cops aren't going to gloss over this, are they?"

"No, Chief Woods is serious about this. The whole Harvest of Praise complex has had a lot of tempers flaring for a long time. He said he wasn't surprised at the fire."

"You mean he's been expecting something like this? Why didn't he say anything?"

"Not expecting." Clarice leans back against the wall. I cringe when I realize she's leaning up against a white board with future story ideas written in red. I hope her tee is washable. "Just not surprised."

"Does he have any theories?"

Gwen clears her throat. "He said one of the more intense church members. Well, duh. Woods is friends with a bunch of the members, although I don't think he goes there himself. I'm sure he sees the congregation as law-abiding, not trouble-makers."

"Did you tell him about the note on your car?" I'm drilling a hole in Gwen and she obligingly turns red.

"Yes, Amy. For what it's worth, I even gave him the note. And told him you and I both touched it."

"That won't do any good." Clarice shares her great expertise with us. "Written on a computer, printed on white copy paper, you think whoever did this would leave prints? Gloves, definitely gloves."

"You're probably right, Clarice, but if this is the same guy, every bit of evidence helps. While you two were gone I had an interesting chat with Art from the Chamber."

"Why Art?" Clarice has a puzzled look and Gwen says, "The Chamber has been one of the big supporters of the project."

She turns to me. "What did you tell him?"

"Since it's public record now and we'll have a story tomorrow, I told him about the fire and the message. He seemed honestly surprised and horrified."

Gwen shows her surprise. "He should be horrified. This kind of vandalism doesn't make Monroe look good. What else did you tell him?"

I give a synopsis of our conversation. Clarice gives me a funny look. "It sounds a little bit like you threatened him, Amy. What are you thinking to get out of it?"

"A lead? Some cooler heads? I don't know if Art has any idea who did this, but the pro-church people need to collectively put a stop to it. Notes and fires will give them a big black eye and turn their friends and supporters off. They have to police themselves. If Art gets the message out that any more vandalism is going to be all over the paper, at least it will stop. It may even get someone to confess." I look at Gwen. "Does this church believe in shunning?"

"I don't think so, Amy. It's evangelical but pretty mainstream."

"So, what do we do now?" Clarice is the action figure and wants to move on this. Shake up the troops, go talk to people.

"We wait. We let the information seep through the leaders and the congregation. It may take a few days, but somebody's going to say something. You've got the story, Clar."

Something stops me. "Did either of you assign Luis to get a picture?"

The two reporters look at one another. "I didn't..." they say in tandem then Clarice says, "I'll do it now."

"You haven't had anybody come in and clear it up, have you, Gwen?"

She shakes her head. "No, I haven't gotten that far ahead. I need to do it soon, my husband's going to be nuclear." She shivers and I know this isn't a topic she wants to bring up with him.

I reach over and touch her arm. "I am so sorry this happened, Gwen. You didn't and don't deserve it. I hope this public airing will stop this idiot. Why don't you go home, see if you can relax. After Luis is done, do you have someone who can come over and resod?"

"I can find someone. It's short notice but Sally may have a name from the horticulture program at city college." She pauses and her eyes well up. "I'll have to check and see if our homeowner's policy covers this." Her purse lands on my desk with a thump as she paws through it, looking for a note pad, a pen and tissues. A small smile flits across her face. "Maybe I can get those leaky sprinkler heads fixed, too."

Once Gwen's left, Clarice turns her attention to me, Dodson, the surveillance camera, Gunther, Suzy and the Delta doings. "So what did the Sheriff," and I can see the air quotes, "have to say about your evidence? Was he pissed?"

"I wouldn't say pissed. He did wish I hadn't watched it, but he's getting a warrant to go pick it up, probably tomorrow morning. He's hoping his lab guys can pull more information from it, but I don't know. There just isn't much there, except the SUV."

Head slap, then, "Did your friend find the license?"

"She did. It's registered to Rivercity Investigations in Monroe."

"I knew it! The pattern of when the van was there has to be someone watching. But watching what? And why? Do you know anything about them?"

"No. Haven't had a chance what with the arsonist and Gwen's lawn. I'll go do a search now."

Within half an hour she's back at my office door with a cat-and-canary look. "Found 'em. Guess what they handle?"

"Roving spouses? Bad fiancés?"

"Well, yes...and workers' comp cheaters."

CHAPTER THIRTY-SIX

Worker's comp cheaters? Fake injuries? And who do we know in that area who's collecting worker's comp?

"Have they had Gunther under surveillance?"

"The man I talked to wouldn't confirm or deny that Gunther was a subject. I'm going to call the state Worker's Comp people and see if I can confirm it through them. Iffy, if it's still an open case." Clarice rumples her hair. "You know, you've opened the door with Sheriff Dodson with surveillance videos. I'm going to ask him if they could get a warrant for Rivercity's videos as well. It's all at the scene of a murder."

"Good. In the meantime, I'll call the contractor's licensing board and ask them what they know about the problems at the corporation yard. They installed the cameras after the two guys were killed, but they may be more interested in thefts."

My fishing expedition nets me very little. Yes, they've had some thefts at the yard. The biggest thing missing is a Bobcat tractor they used for moving pipes and drills around. Somebody came in in the afternoon, got it started, picked up a load of pipe and drove out. No one reported it, it looked like a normal activity.

Clarice has better luck with Dodson. They've already talked to Rivercity Investigations and have a warrant for the videos shot by the guy in the SUV. The Sheriff will review them, understanding that Rivercity's interest is in catching Gunther doing something physical he shouldn't be doing with a disability.

Are we invited to the screening? "Ha, not a chance." Clarice says and gives me a look. "Maybe if you hadn't...."

"Don't go there, Clarice. You know we'd never have been invited to watch those, even without my, my..."

"Interference? Is that the word you're looking for?" She blows out a huff. "I know. Though I would have done the same thing if I'd found out about them."

We're quiet for a beat, then Mark Cruz pops into my head.

"I forgot to tell you, when I was leaving Cruz's house, he asked about Suzy. He said, 'With Gunter in jail, do you think she might move back here?'"

A big grin blooms on Clarice's face. "You're kidding! That's an amazing thing. I wonder if they had something going."

"I doubt it. Cruz knew what Gunther was like. He told me that none of the neighbors would cross Gunther, they steered clear. I think he felt sorry for Suzy and the more he saw her situation, the more he was interested. It may have been a white knight kind of thing, rescuing a damsel from a dragon."

"I wonder if she knows?" The blond has a slightly dreamy look.

"Are you planning to tell her? Have you seen her since she's been at the shelter?"

"I talked to her once. She's still having a hard time getting around on crutches but her ribs are healing. The doctors think she'll need some cosmetic surgery for her face, but that can come later."

A speculative gleam is in her eye. "Maybe I'll go visit her this evening."

Hmmm, should I have told her about Cruz' possible interest? "Don't go off on Suzy. This is just an idle thought. After all, with Gunther facing a good-sized prison sentence, the house is just sitting empty. I'm sure Cruz would want to see someone living in it. He's already had vandalism problems when he's gone."

A sliver of something whips through my brain too fast to catch hold of. I close my eyes, urging the synapses to recreate their travels and it comes to me. "The house is sitting empty. Suzy may not want to move back, unless it's her house. Who owns it?"

If it's in both their names—and it could be if Gunther wanted her to go down with him on the cultivation charges—she could divorce him and end up with the title.

"I'll ask her. I want to talk to her about a divorce, anyway. This time, she's ready, I think." Clarice gathers up her notepad, purse, sunglasses, phone and heads out. "I'm off to the city cops to see if they have anything on Gwen's fire."

I call the Public Information Officer at the Department of Industrial Relations. I'm not sure they'll tell me if they have an open case on Gunther, but I'm in luck. They've been watching him and are about to slap an administrative suit against him. After I tell the PIO about Gunther's other activities and arrest, she says, "Just a minute." I'm on tacky hold music then she's back. "I passed on your information to the investigator on the case. We'll probably add fraud charges. Thanks for letting us know."

The Workers' Comp people had an active case open and didn't know Gunther'd been arrested on attempted murder charges? Well, they're part of a big bureaucracy and I doubt if they cull through local arrest records daily.

I'm at a lull. Gwen's gone home to meet with a landscaper after finding out her homeowners' policy will cover a new lawn. There's the usual hum of the newsroom, low-voice phone conversations, keyboards clicking. I pull up the local stories and begin copy-reading those slotted for tomorrow's paper, but my mind drifts back to the bulldozer clearing the lot where the meth house was in my neighborhood.

A flash, then I call the sheriff's department and ask for either Krutz or Wilkes. They hadn't asked about any other drug activity in the area, focusing on Gunther and the Delta, but I wonder if they have any leads on the Arizona absentee landlord.

"Just call me Harry" picks up and I ask him my question.

"We did talk to the owner," Wilkes says. "He claimed that he didn't know what the renter was doing. He's not happy the house was razed, but, oh well. We're working with the Phoenix DEA office to keep an eye on him."

If I'd been talking to Krutz I probably wouldn't ask my transportation question, but Wilkes seems like a straight-shooter so I run Gunther's travel patterns by him. At least as much as I know them.

I can hear a smile in his voice. "I'm beginning to see why Sheriff Dodson talks to you so much, Ms. Hobbes. You think like someone in law enforcement."

Now I'm smiling. "Part of it is just the nosy reporter. Part of it is that I love puzzles. But a big part is from my first husband," and I give him a shortened version of Vinnie. He offers condolences and I understand that he's seeing me as part of the law enforcement family, one of the reasons Jim Dodson and I are close.

"As far as Mohre's travel patterns, we did look at his logs, mileage, stops. He was inspected at a station once, but they didn't find anything. He's been out on disability so long that he's dropped off the load inspection radar." Wilkes pauses, then, "From his logs in the past, we thought he took the long routes for some deliveries, but nothing overt."

My mouth is moving before I can put any filters in place. "Then why did you show up in Monroe when you did? It feels like you brought a bunch of drug searches with you."

Oops. That's probably going to tick him off. I quietly suck in a breath.

Instead, there's a low laugh on the other end. "You don't believe in subtlety, do you? We've been looking at several of these things individually, then the murders of the workers at the corporation yard made us rethink. So much activity centered around a small spot...we wanted to take a look. Then when Mohre's wife ended up in the hospital..."

"Suzy. Her name's Suzy." I hate that they're reducing her to the wife of a sleaze.

He's silent for a beat. "You're right, her name is Suzy. She doesn't deserve the treatment she's gotten."

"You people aren't looking at her as having any part in the drugs, are you?"

"No, not now." Wilkes sounds sort of ashamed. "Initially, we wondered if they were a team, but it's clear that whatever Mohre was doing, he did it alone."

Small consolation for Suzy.

CHAPTER THIRTY-SEVEN

Gwen's back at work and on the phone this morning. I wave at her and point to my office. I have the local budget of stories up when she knocks and comes in.

"I wasn't sure I'd see you today. If you need to take a day off, that's fine."

"Thanks, Amy, but I couldn't stay in that house any more. Waiting for someone to show up and throw a bomb or something."

"Oh!" My mouth falls open. "I didn't think that through. Were you frightened last night?"

She has a slightly haunted look. "No, I called a friend. She came and stayed with me."

"And your husband's coming home today?"

Gwen nods.

I wait. Silence. "Have you told him yet?"

She nods again.

This is like picking unripe oranges. I have to tug. "What did he say?"

"He wasn't happy."

There's a niggling at the back of my neck. "He wouldn't be mad at you, would he? Would he hurt you?"

Her eyes open so wide her forehead wrinkles. "No...no, Amy. He'd never touch me."

"Well, how angry was he?"

"He yelled at me on the phone about 'That stupid job.' He said it isn't worth this kind of aggravation or danger."

"How do you feel about it?" People have dropped out of the news business from a lot less pressure than this. I'd hate to see Gwen go, she's solid, reliable and has been at the *Press* long enough that she carries corporate memory. With the turnover in young, green reporters, she's the one they can go to for the basics in how Monroe works, and with whom.

She smiles but I see a trace of sadness behind her eyes. "Yes, I think it's worth aggravation. Maybe not at this level." I watch her organizing her thoughts. "I like being in the know about the way city hall works. It's interesting to follow somebody from the time they're first elected to when they've accumulated enough seniority to make changes."

I understand what she means. People come in to office on the promise of changing things. It takes them a while—a few months to a few years—to figure out how the system works. How you can find consensus, how you build coalitions, how you curry votes. And the big lesson, what power staffers hold and what power elected officials hold.

"Does this mean you're staying?" My mental fingers are crossed.

"I'm staying for now, Amy."

"Good. I know how hard it is to balance your family's wishes with your need to stay. The city hall beat may not give you the cops' adrenaline, but there is excitement." I'm quiet for a second or two. "What can I do to help you with this? You know you can tell your husband any of my story about Vinnie. There's always risk around. Look at those guys who turn into workplace shooters. People say 'I had no idea, he was so quiet and polite.'"

I manage to get a real smile from her now.

"Thanks, but he'll get over it. He mostly doesn't like change, even gets grumpy when I work a late shift to cover elections or late night meetings."

I've met Gwen's husband, Gil, and he doesn't strike me as the type who wants dinner on the table at six every night. "Is he rigid about your hours?"

"Not rigid, no. It's just when we're together he doesn't want work to interfere. I do a flip of my mental switch when I'm heading in or heading home."

I stare at her. This ability to even have a switch is why I like hiring women. We're always multitasking. I once heard someone (male) describe a woman's thought processes as like having multiple screens constantly open on your computer. It only takes a second to move from one to another. The response was that it must get tiring. It does, sometimes.

"I'm glad you're staying. You'd be sorely missed. Now, let's figure out how to handle this."

I have to pull her off the vandalism story, and may give some of the research and reporting of Harvest of Praise's contract with the city to someone else. It can't be the religion reporter, Roberts, he wouldn't see anything wrong. The education reporter, Sally, is my next best bet and I send her a note to see me.

Gwen says, "I need to start returning phone calls. I've gotten a stack of them this morning. So far, they're apologies and condolences for the arson."

It's what I was hoping for. If the vandal is a member of the congregation they wouldn't give us a name, but they could band together to put pressure on the arsonist or the family.

As Gwen gets up to leave, Sally comes through the door. I motion Gwen to stay. I need to talk to them together. I see handing off this story as a temporary measure, only until the threat blows over. To do this right, they both have to be in the loop on information and sources. I particularly need Gwen to hand over her phone calls and sources.

When I say this, both reporters look stunned. Sources are confidential, not shared with anyone. "I'm not asking either of you to breech your relationships. Just share enough information, Gwen, so Sally can ask intelligent questions."

Sally's read Gwen's stories on the possible collusion between Harvest of Praise and the city so she knows the gist. It takes a few minutes for her to get filled in on the players and the current events. I'm wondering if the anti forces have met and talked about their next move. Gwen believes they have—and the next move is a suit to halt any further discussion until the street change matter is resolved.

This will be Sally's assignment while Gwen returns calls and gives callers Sally's contact information. While they're hitting the phones, I look at my own pink drift of notes. Hmmm, there are three from Art at the Chamber, so I start with him.

"Has there been any other damage?" He doesn't mince words, goes right for the heart of the matter. More damage means another story, means another black eye for Monroe, means he'll catch flak. Compassion is his middle name?

"No, Art, no more arson. I don't think the police are any closer to catching the guy, though. What have you heard?"

This seems to take the oxygen away. Art gasps, stammers, says, "Uh, oh, hmmm..." before finally settling for "Nothing." He adds, "I have had a lot of calls from congregation members. I heard they've called a meeting for tonight."

"Tonight?" My brain is turning over ways to get a reporter to the meeting when he says, "Well, it's not a public meeting, just some of the members getting together to discuss things."

Good save. We'd have to have a personal invitation to go to the meeting now and I doubt we're pals enough with any of the church people that they'd ask us in for coffee.

I stare out my office window at the newsroom, running in idle until I bolt for the library.

CHAPTER THIRTY-EIGHT

Nancy. She's more than just the research librarian, she belongs to a lot of clubs around town. I know she's not a member of the Harvest of Praise, but I'd bet she knows people who are.

It's too early for lunch so I dangle buying her a latte to lure her out. She takes the bait and we walk to a small coffee shop in the next block. It hasn't hit ninety degrees yet and we can sit outside. I don't know if I'm going to be asking her to divulge any great secrets, but being outside means people won't linger to talk to either of us.

"I know you're not buying coffee because I'm so attractive." She smooths her hair and raises an eyebrow. "What's the deal?"

I tell her about subbing Sally for Gwen on following the church-city mélange and then, "Some church members are meeting tonight to 'discuss' things."

"And you found this out, how?"

"Pffttt...you know my sources are confidential, Nancy." Pause. "I talked to Art at the Chamber."

She laughs so hard it looks like she's liable to choke. After a minute or so, she wipes her eyes on a napkin. "I'm going to have to fix my makeup before I go back to work. Boy, I certainly hope nobody wants to subpoena your notes, Amy. I can see that you'd never go to jail for protecting a source."

"You may be right, but Art is only one of many who knows about the meeting. Hell, he may be planning to go. My problem is either how to get Sally in, or how to find out what gets talked about from someone who's there. Since it's not a public event, just a group of people getting together privately to talk about an issue, the only way Sally, or Gwen or I for that matter, can go is to be invited. And after the barbecue on Gwen's lawn, that isn't going to happen."

"Yeah, I don't think the *Press* is on the A-list for parties with that group. So what's your Plan B?"

"I thought you might know who's going."

Nancy slides her sunglasses down her nose and looks at me as though I've grown a second head. "Are you crazy? You can't crash the party so you want me to?"

"No, not crash the party. Just ask around a little and see if you can give us some names of who's going. Sally can call them tomorrow and ask how the meeting went."

"Do you really think they'll talk to her?"

"I don't know. Most of them probably won't, but this would be their chance to get their side of the story out."

She takes a sip of her drink, maybe giving herself time to respond. "Their side of the deal with the city, or their side of the threats against Gwen?"

I shrug. "Either? Both? We've had a lot of calls...many of them not very nice. Gwen still hasn't had a formal response from the church board about the deal with the city. And I'd love to find out if they're doing anything to find and rein in the vandal who set the fire. If they're smart, they'll find him themselves and turn him over to the cops. That one action was a body blow to all the positive PR they've been trying to build."

"I know. You'd think they'd keep all their folks muzzled with a political issue this hot." Nancy shakes her head. "I can't figure out people who persist in shooting themselves in the foot."

Fine, she agrees with me. Now, will she help me find a spy, a rat, a tattler? "Do you know anyone who might be going tonight?" Blatant, but I'm up against a time constraint here.

"I might. Josie's husband is heavily involved. I'll call her and invite her for a drink. If they're going to the meeting, she'll say no." She pushes her glasses up again. "I heard that Heather was in town last weekend. Everything alright?"

Back on our common ground, I give her a rundown of Heather's new house and moving plans. "I'm thinking in a month or so, when she's settled, I'll have a barbecue-swim party, get some of the kids together."

She laughs. "Kids? You living in some time-warp land? They're not kids any more, some even *have* kids."

"Whatever, I'll probably go to my grave thinking of them as high school kids. I know Heather stayed in touch with a few of them and they'd like to know she's back in the area."

"Don't you think she'd rather ask them herself? To see her new house? Hear about her new job?"

I look at Nancy. When did she get so wise?

She grins. "Remember, I'm a grandmother now. I've had to let mine grow up and leave the nest."

Bingo. She's right, again. "It's hard not being Mom, but I'll tell her she can use my house for the get-together if she'd like."

I check my phone for the time and find a message from Clarice, "Need to talk. At the Sheriff's office. Call. Come over."

"Oops, gotta run. Now Clarice is holding meetings at Jim Dodson's office. That sounds ominous."

Nancy smiles, gathers up her things and we walk back. "You'll call me if you find anyone going tonight?"

"I will. But don't hold your breath. This might be a quiet little gathering to keep the lid on." She waves and disappears into the air conditioning of the building. I wonder what it would be like to go to work every day in a calm, serene place, even if they don't have big "Silence" signs up any more. Then I remember that one of the suburban branches has security guards. More for theft than mayhem but it's still a portent of the times.

I swing by the newsroom to tell Sally and Gwen that Nancy will put out feelers for a contact at tonight's meeting. They've been busy working the phones, both to look for attendees themselves and for Gwen to introduce Sally as the new lead reporter.

"I've had half a dozen people tell me not to give up on the story," Gwen says. "The ones who like that we've uncovered the city money, of course. Although I even had a call from one of the bigger supporters. He said not to let one out-of-control jerk scare me off. 'If there's a problem with city money in the project, it needs to come to light.' Pretty enlightened response, I thought."

Sally nods. "Three of the calls I returned to tell them I was on the story now were very civil. One said, 'I know you're just doing your job and it's not a personal attack against the church.' Surprised me."

"Thanks, guys. I'm going over to the Sheriff's office. Need to find out what's up with Clarice."

Gwen says, "We'll call you if Nancy gives us any names."

The brief time in the cool office was good. Now I'm back out in the heat again for the short walk to Jim Dodson's.

How does Clarice manage to call a meeting at his office?

CHAPTER THIRTY-NINE

As I walk through the front door of the Sheriff's Department, the receptionist waves me over. "They're all back in the small conference room," she says quietly.

This was why both the Sheriff and the police used regular officers on reception duty, part of an administrative rotation. With budget cut-backs, they've put all the sworn officers on the street and filled in most of the admin jobs with civilians. The lower pay scale, helps offset the cost of refitting the receptionist's area with bullet-proof glass and a small pass-through drawer. The down side is that it makes me feel as though I'm visiting someone in jail.

I'm buzzed through, just another reason that Clarice uses the back employee entrance when she can.

The small conference room is dark, but there are voices so I tap and go in. Jim Dodson is there with Clarice and two guys I don't know and they have a video up on the screen.

"Hi, Amy. Come look what we've found." Dodson's voice is jolly. This must be a good thing. "Wait a minute, this is Lui and Bevans. They're from our forensic IT department."

The techs pull themselves away from the keyboard and monitor where they're manipulating images and nod at me. I nod back. Forensic IT guys? Maybe they did find more on Cruz' video than I thought. I'm about to say something when Clarice can't contain herself any more. She's all but jumping up and down and is practically inarticulate.

"Look, look!" She's pointing at the large image on the screen.

I look. It's a big, a really big, fuzzy ball.

"What am I looking at?" I suspect it's a person, but it could be a galaxy far, far away for all that I can identify. "Is this Mark Cruz' video?"

Dodson shakes his head. "Nope this is video from Rivercity. The PI company?"

"Is that Gunther?"

"No, Amy, that's a guy in the corporation yard!" Clarice could be viewing an Oscar contender from the excitement in her voice.

I turn to the Sheriff. "I'm confused. I thought Rivercity was watching Gunther for the disability claim."

"They were; this may be collateral gold." Even Dodson has a lift to his voice. "They had one investigator stationed in an SUV—the one Cruz's camera caught. Those videos are all aimed at Gunther and his house. But they also had a permanently mounted camera on the dashboard. That runs all the time. It's a wider angle and ended up with some footage of the corporation yard."

The corporation yard? Cameras were installed after the murders. This must be one of the most filmed places in the state.

Dodson sees the question on my face. "Sure, they installed cameras, but this video is date-stamped *before* the murders and thefts."

"So you're saying you may have video of the thief?" This is pretty spiffy but doesn't seem a big enough revelation for all the excitement.

"Not just the thefts, Amy. I've asked Lui and Bevans to isolate the footage from the time of the murders."

My jaw drops. Now I understand why Clarice is acting like she's run across fire ants. Is he telling me that they may have video of the actual murder?

"Are you telling me you might have video of the actual murder?"

Dodson smiles. "Don't get too excited, Amy." He points to Clarice. "She's excited enough for both of you...for all of us. We don't know what we have. Right now they've found video of the yard and a person. I want to see if there's enough information in the image to identify him. If we can, then it's worthwhile going back to the murder dates."

I'm trying to cram all of this in my head and make sense of it. If there was a guy with a camera taking video of Gunther, how could he miss seeing something going on in the corporation yard?

When I ask Dodson, he frowns. "The investigator was focused on Gunther. He's the object of the surveillance. The only reason the dash camera caught anything is that it's a wider-angle lens. And what it caught, looked at with normal resolution, really looks like a big blob of lint. Plus, that part of the yard is probably a good fifty yards away from Gunther's house."

"Fine." I'm not arguing exactly, just needing more clarification. This explanation isn't much clearer than the fuzzy blob. "It's just weird that there may be a lot of information that no one ever looked at."

I get a nod from the Sheriff. "That's one of the problems with surveillance video. There can be so much information that you focus on the immediate, the close shot, and the background can get overlooked. We never would have gotten this video, or looked at it closely, without you bringing Mark Cruz and the SUV to our attention."

A slow warmth glows in my stomach area and spreads. I never started out to find a murderer or abrogate anything law enforcement was doing, but it's nice to be recognized for my help. Particularly from the local sheriff. Too often, it's a competition, not a sharing exercise.

"So, OK, now that we know it's a person, what's next?" I appreciate Dodson's excitement. I doubt this blob will help in any sort of line-up, though.

"We're going to go back over all of Rivercity's video." My question drags Lui away from manipulating the keyboard. "Now we know that the yard is visible, we'll check all the surveillance. This is the part of our work that we call job security. Tedious, but necessary." He grins at me. A techie with a sense of humor. I'm nosy by nature, but forever glad I don't have this job.

"How long will this take?" It's immaterial, just a question to fill the gap of silence.

"Could be a few days." Bevans looks back at me. "If we can focus just on the small portion of the yard, it might go fast."

I glance at Dodson. He's riveted on the screen, looking as though he could will the information to appear. He feels me and turns. "Yes, Amy. You're part of this and I'll call you when and if we find anything."

Then the waves of resentment rolling off Clarice must have hit him in the head. "And Clarice, you're a big part of this as well. I promise I'll keep you in the loop."

I doubt that this was what she wanted to hear, but it seems to mollify her. At least her grim expression softens, she gives Dodson a small smile and says, "Thanks."

As Clarice and I are leaving, I ask, "Have Krutz and Wilkins found anything more on Gunther's travels?"

He tears his attention away from the video, looks at me with a blank expression. "Travels?" Silence. Then, "Oh, his driving logs. They haven't pinned down a place yet, but almost every trip has an unscheduled stop between here and his ultimate destination. He didn't cover it up well, probably didn't think he needed to since he's an owner operator and doesn't show anyone his logs."

"How did they find the stops, then? If Gunther wasn't writing things down, would there be a trace of where he went?"

"His time and mileage. He kept mileage for the IRS, and the trips took up to four hours longer that they should have." Dodson smiles at me. "You may not like the state people, but they are investigators, Amy. They know how to figure things out."

CHAPTER FORTY

Clarice and I are wrapped in our own thoughts on the walk back to the office.

She finally says, "I need to weed through and throw out some red herrings. There're just too many pieces that don't fit. They're sticking around, getting in the way."

"Good idea, Want any help?" I have some of those pieces myself.

"Sure. Is this a good time?"

I wave her into my office then have second thoughts. "Let's go downstairs. If we're out of sight of the others, we may be out of mind." We grab an armload of notebooks, a handful of whiteboard markers and head out. In the small room, we drop everything on the table and I write, breaking our hunt to-date down to "Delta," "Drugs," "Gunther" and "Suzy".

We each list our facts under the categories and after a few minutes, sit back and look at what we have.

"I think one thing we can throw out is the Posse and conspiracy theorists." Clarice wipes them off under the

"Delta" list. She's right, they were an interesting, scary idea, but we haven't found anything to link them to events.

"What about the guy in Arizona? The absentee landlord? He may have been a link to Mexican drug cartels, but I can't put him into the Delta puzzle. I think we should leave him to the CHP and DEA guys." Clarice nods in agreement.

I'm quiet for a bit, staring at what's left on the lists we've made. "As much as I liked them, we can throw out the anti-tunnel crowd as well. They're upset, but from my conversations with and about them, they're using a legal way to stop eminent domain. I don't think anyone who has the patience to file a suit would resort to murder."

"You know if we take all those out-of-area ideas and toss them, we're left with a couple of local murders and a nasty piece of work who beats up his wife."

"Right, a small-time, scummy character who chisels the disability folks and makes problems for his neighbors."

We look at each other and crack up. With the tension of the last few days, Gunther's arrest, the surveillance of the corporation yard, possibly getting the murders on video, we laugh. "This isn't much different than our hide-a-bed drug thugs." Clarice catches her breath.

"Yeah, but we had a lot of fun building those air castles. And we still don't know who murdered those construction workers—or when or with what. It could still be Gunther. They could have seen his garden and tried blackmail for a piece of the action."

"And what?" She's trying to see the blackmail angle. "Is that enough for him to murder them? Two of them? He lashes out in anger, but I don't see him being calm enough to calculate two attacks."

I pick up the eraser and clean the boards. "Well, we still have the videos. We can hope the techs get enough information that there's a chance of identifying someone."

We gather up stuff and she says, "One other thing. I met with Suzy. This will be a great story...maybe even a book."

"A book? There are an awful lot of books about battered women."

"I know. But it still goes on. The victims still feel they face stigmas and embarrassment."

Hmmm...there are lots of journalists who write books about the stories they cover, and a few who write books and never cover things. I hadn't put Clarice in the book-writing club. "What would you do with the money?"

Both of us laugh. There probably won't be any money. Writing books these days isn't a moneymaking proposition, although a non-fiction about an issue like battered women is bound to sell better than a murder mystery from some unknown writer.

"Ha, you're funny! I wouldn't write it to make money. I want to get more information out about domestic abuse, child abuse, sexual assault...all those acts of violence against the people closest to you. I have such a hard time wrapping my head around it." She's pensive. "If there were any money, though, I'd probably donate most of it to a shelter program."

Just like when she told me the story of her friend Angie, there are things I don't know about Clarice. When I think she has her hard-boiled reporter shell on, she'll amaze me with her compassion.

We climb the stairs to the newsroom and I say, "That's a great idea. If you do decide to write a book, I'll work with you all the way."

She turns to me, a step behind her, and gives me such an impish grin I wonder if she made the book story up to gain my interest or sympathy. At the question in my eyes, she shakes her head. "I'm not kidding about this, Amy. Some day..." She trails off and I hope her some day comes sooner than my plan to write a book about another of our major stories. Three people ended up dead when Senator Robert Calvert, a local who became a WWII hero, and U.S. Senator was revealed to have stolen a da Vinci drawing.

When she checks her desk, there's a message to call Lt. Greene of the Monroe city cops. I can see her on the phone, hear her say, "I'll be right over," and watch her come toward me.

"Yes?"

"Not a whole lot, but they did get some tips on the arsonist."

"That's good news. Anyone we know?"

"Greene wouldn't say anything on the phone. I'm thinking these are only tips and he doesn't expect they'll pan out. It's worth a trip over there, though."

"I agree. Do you want me to tell Gwen?"

She purses her lips. Taps her sunglasses against them. "Noooo, I don't think so. Not until I have a chance to check it out. There's no sense getting her hopes up."

Good. Gwen's been through enough. I need to talk to her, though.

I walk over to her cubicle. She's on the phone and her end of the conversation sounds business-like. "You'll sign-off on the claim and we can get started tomorrow?" The other end must have agreed because Gwen says, "Thanks for your help."

She turns, sees me and gives a little jump. "Amy, I didn't know you were there. Did you want to see me?"

"I was wondering how you are. Have you heard from your homeowner's insurance? Will they cover a new lawn?"

"Yes, that was my adjuster on the phone. Because it was so visible, and because the police are involved, and because we ran a story on it, it's so documented that they couldn't say no. Now I have to call the landscapers and get them set up for tomorrow."

The business part of this disaster was coming together but the personal cost?

"How's Gil taking all this? Is he still upset?"

"He's calmed down a little. He's not raging at me about quitting. In fact, he's told his boss that he doesn't want so many business trips, he wants to spend more time here, at the main office." Gil works for a company that manufactures irrigation piping and their products are in demand as water deliveries from the federal water projects get cut back. Gone are the days of farmers flooding their fields.

"That's good...isn't it?"

Gwen smiles. "Yep, that's good."

Odd bedfellows. The drought and an angry arsonist have pulled this couple closer together.

CHAPTER FORTY-ONE

Next morning I'm skimming the San Francisco paper when my landline rings with a local number and "unidentified caller." I let those go to voicemail. If they know me, they'll either leave a message or call my cell.

The caller is beginning to leave a message when I grab the phone. "Hey, Jim, sorry I didn't pick up."

There's a short laugh as the Sheriff says "Monitoring your calls?"

"I won't pick up unless it's a name or number I know. People can find me at the paper if they want to talk to me."

"Yep, the down side of celebrity status. Or maybe notoriety. Did I catch you at a bad time?"

A bad time? Why is Jim Dodson calling me at eight-thirty in the morning on a work day? And what number is he calling from? "No, not bad. I'm headed to the shower. What's up? Where are you calling from?"

"From home. On a landline. I don't use it for work as a rule, but don't want this call traced."

"You're making me nervous."

"Don't mean to. Wondering if you can swing by my office before you go in. I have something I'd like you to look at."

This is all a little mysterious. Dodson is usually a straight-up kind of guy. "Sure. It'll be about half an hour."

"See you then." Not a good-bye, just a hang-up.

I pound upstairs, spend five minutes in the shower raising and rejecting ideas—Gwen's lawn fire, the meth house, Gunther, the tunnel crowd? None of these are topics that should make Dodson hesitant to talk.

Grab a linen sundress, throw on some make-up, slip into sandals and I'm at Dodson's office in thirty-one minutes. It pays to live close to your work.

What I haven't had time for is my second cup of coffee, but the Sheriff takes care of that, detouring into the break room to pour me a cup as he herds me to the conference room. I nod at Lui and Bevens, Dodson flips the lights off and I'm staring at a face on the big screen.

In truth, it's not much of a picture. Fuzzy, just an outline with a few visible features. Heavy eyebrows, receding hairline, ears close to the head, bulbous nose. No clue what color eyes or hair. Could be any age from maybe thirty to sixty.

"Does he look familiar?" Dodson's voice is flat, no inflections.

"You have to be kidding! This could be a picture of anybody. The original 'average'."

"I know. I'm sorry, but this is the best we could get from the video." He turns to Lui. "Put the others up."

A series of nine faces lines up on the screen, this time mug shots, maybe from licenses.

"Any of these?"

I squinch my eyes, trying to put the faces into some context. "No, I don't know those men...wait...that one on the upper left. I've seen him somewhere." I narrow my gaze and a hot day comes to me...a hot day and dust.

"He's the one I spoke to at the corporation yard the day I met Mark Cruz. Who are these guys?"

"These are the employees Earth/Search's using to do the core sampling. They all work in and out of the corporation yard."

The faces stare back at me, impassive, almost resigned. "What are these? They almost look like booking photos."

This gets a laugh from Dodson. "No, these are their work IDs. Earth/Search has contracts with the state, so employees are required to pass a background screen and wear photo badges."

"There are only nine here. Is the company that small?"

"Earth/Search is a mid-sized company. This is the crew assigned to the Delta core drilling. At that, they're down by two. These two," he points to a man in the bottom row and one on the right, "are the murder victims."

A shivery feeling runs across my scalp. I've looked at tons of booking photos, mug shots of dead people, even autopsy shots, but something about these two faces is uncomfortable.

"When I was out there talking to that guy," I point at the one on the top left, "he said they were short-handed because of the murders."

"What else did he say? I know you were there before you talked to Cruz, but I haven't asked what you saw in the yard."

I cast my mind back. The day is hot. The equipment storage area is only bulldozed dirt, compacted enough to drive the trucks on. A fine haze of silty dust rises from my footsteps and the dust outlines the man coming toward me. When he spots me, he yells.

"First, he told me I couldn't be there, their insurance carrier wouldn't like the liability. When I asked if he knew the dead guys, he got quiet...kind of withdrawn. He said he didn't know them well, just co-workers."

"That's it?"

I replay the conversation. "He said something about the crew being sloppy, not putting their tools away. Seemed miffed that he had to pick up after them."

Dodson is silent for a beat, then, "Pick up what?"

"Tools, just tools...oh my god." I'm remembering the big wrench in the man's hand. The nervousness that rippled over me.

"What?" Dodson sees I've found something.

"He was walking toward me, carrying this wrench. I flashed that the two workers were killed with a blunt object and wondered if this was it. Then he tossed it in the truck."

"In the back or the front?"

"No, into one of those big tool chest things on the side of the truck bed."

He's making notes, asks Lui if he can superimpose the man I identified over the fuzzy picture.

When the tech is finished, I gasp.

"That's him. That's the guy I talked to."

Dodson smiles. "I thought it might have been. We need to have a chat with him, take a look at his truck and tools. Thanks for coming in so early, Amy."

Wait until I tell Clarice! Oops, wait a minute. "What can I tell Clarice?"

"Nothing yet, please. I'll have one of my deputies call her after we bring this guy in."

"You're going to arrest him?" Am I a witness in a murder investigation now? I don't like this.

"Not arrest, just talk. We need to get enough for a search warrant for his house and truck."

A warrant. I have a funny feeling up my spine as I walk to the *Press*. Do I have a target on my back?

CHAPTER FORTY-TWO

The call from the sheriff's deputy comes in before Clarice has a chance to drop her stuff. I watch her face as she hears the news then can't even count to three by the time she's in my office.

"Amy, they're pulling a guy in to question about the Delta murders! It's one of the construction workers. They found the murders on the video that the Rivercity surveillance PI shot. A person who'd talked to the construction worker identified him on the video."

She shakes her head. "After all of our theories, all of the possible conspiracies, it's probably one of the co-workers. Wonder what sent him over the edge?"

"Who knows, Clar. Go and find out for us. And the murders on video? What are the odds of that?"

"I know," trails out of the blond as she heads out at a fast walk for the Sheriff's office. "I'll call."

Is it right that I haven't said anything to her?

Yes. She may be pissed when she finds out I'm the witness, but she'll understand. Also, now they know they have the murder on video, they'll be able to find someone else who saw something.

It feels flat, though. After all our questions, all our suppositions, two men died because a co-worker was angry. Murder is a tawdry crime, boiling down to greed or sex. I wonder which these killings are.

I'll find out as soon as Clarice gets back. In the meantime, Gwen and Sally are tag-teaming me at my door, elbowing to be the first to tell me.

"You owe your friend Nancy a dinner or something." Gwen's first.

"Yeah." Sally's an immediate next. "Her tip about who might be at the church meeting was spot on."

"So tell," I look from one excited face to the other.

"We each called some of our regular sources who Nancy said might be there." Sally has a big grin. "Even some of my school people were there." It's not often that the school beat yields breaking news, let alone information about a crime.

"We don't have a name," Gwen breaks in, "but they said they did talk about who burned my lawn."

My eyes widen. "The congregation knows who the vandal is? This had better get to the cops."

Gwen looks stunned. "We can't tell the cops! They'd know where we heard it and we weren't there. I don't think the whole congregation knows, anyway. Mar..." She slams a hand over her mouth. "Uhhh, one of the callers said they thought it was a teen-aged son of a...member."

Peeling the onion again. Layers under layers under layers. I shake my head. "Not a lot to go on. What else did the 'sources' have to say?"

"A lot of the church leaders were at the meeting, several from the board." Sally looks at her notes, then glances back up at me. "Well, names don't matter so much. Everybody there was upset. They're going to send a delegation to talk to the boy's parents. My source said they've had some problems with him in the past."

"Problems?"

Gwen takes a breath. "Apparently they asked him to leave a youth group. He was pushing for separating the boys and girls and upset at the secular tone of the music. Thought that Christian rock was inappropriate."

That could be a big problem if what Art told me about Harvest of Praise positioning itself as a venue on the Christian touring schedule is true. Those touring groups bring in several thousand people each program, money the congregation can use.

"What are the next steps?" I look from Gwen to Sally.

"The group, maybe the board, wants to talk to the family, counsel them. They didn't mention anything else. It would really blindside them to have a police investigation." Sally seems like she'd like to keep the cops out as well.

"One of my sources said they planned to talk to the family, get the boy to apologize to me and do community service work." From her expression, Gwen would like to pretend this whole thing never happened, but it's too late to stuff this genie back in the bottle.

"Eventually the cops have to find this out. We know there's a line from arson to serious crimes against people...usually torture and murder."

Sally sucks in a quiet breath and Gwen pales. Have I told them something they don't know? No, they're uncomfortable with the idea of a serial killer growing up in Monroe.

"I know we don't have a name." I do a laser stare at each of them. "If you do have a name, I don't want to hear it. We can hold off talking to the cops until the boy's parents have a chance to handle it."

Eventually, the city police will have to find out. Sally and Gwen can work with congregation members so they can figure out how to tell the cops. The kid will end up doing time in juvenile hall. I'm hoping he'll get some heavy-duty psychiatric counseling as well. I'd feel ecstatic if I had a hand in finding and stopping a potential killer.

"Let me know when you hear anything else." I smile. "Good work you two."

Gwen waves her hand in a "nada" motion. "We didn't do that much, it's Nancy's contacts that got us here."

"True. And I owe her a dinner at least." I pick up my purse, wave Sally and Gwen out of my office and brave the heat for a short walk to the library.

It's hard to lure Nancy out of her air-conditioning but an iced latte does it. I wait until we have our drinks and settle at a quiet back table.

"A couple of people think I owe you a dinner. I'm on the cheap, though. Besides, we can't pay our sources."

She laughs. "I'm guessing from your convoluted comments that I was some help."

"You were." I fill her in on the conversation.

"Ouch. I sure don't want to know who it is. That's a tragedy waiting to happen. Those parents must be horrified."

I nod. "I was hoping my talk with Art would shake some things loose. I'm not happy that it might be a kid involved."

"You can't take any responsibility for learning who it was." Nancy's career at the library gives her a great understanding into the hearts and minds of people as she watches, day-to-day.

"Monroe may be a small town, but it's a microcosm of the world."

She grins. "Remember Miss Marple? She never moved from St. Mary Mead."

CHAPTER FORTY-THREE

Only Nancy could compare Monroe with St. Mary Mead. The image tickles me. We may be a small town, but we share big city problems with the larger places surrounding us. This hits home when Clarice comes back from the sheriff.

She's back. And she's miffed.

"From the look on your face, I'm guessing Sheriff Dodson told you I'm the witness."

Serious stink-eye rolls off her. "Yes."

One-word answers. This isn't good. "I couldn't tell you. I've ended up the only one who can tie the fuzzy blob in the video to a real person. I'm not happy being involved in whatever's going on...thefts, murder..." I shrug and blow out a sigh.

"I wish you'd have said *something*, Amy. I felt like a lump of fish bait, ready to get fed to the sharks."

Her imagery is good, even if off the mark. "This had nothing to do with you, Clarice. The information had to come from Sheriff Dodson."

I'm quiet for a beat, then, "When we were sorting information yesterday, we came to the conclusion that the deaths were just tatty little murders. In the meantime the sheriff's been partially taken over by the state cops and probably a DEA team is in the wings. If my identification of the murderer impinges on any of this wide-scale drug investigation, I'm toast as a journalist. I pulled Gwen off the Harvest of Praise street financing story. I don't want me, or the *Press*, to be pulled off the Delta mess."

This doesn't stand the test of an apology, but then I don't owe her one. I do want to give her some explanation. She still has the murders to write and wants to continue on the Suzy/Gunther story. There are plenty of worms in this bait can to follow. I don't want to muddy the waters if she got some information or identification from a witness who happens to be her boss.

I close my eyes. This is giving me a headache.

Clarice is humming something under her breath that might be a Cold Play song. It's covering for her while she sorts out whether to be mad or conciliatory and the latter wins, thank you. Working with Clarice and keeping the friend/boss lines straight is hard enough without resentment and anger.

"OK, Amy, I understand. It just came as a shock when the Sheriff told me they had a witness who could identify the murderer from the surveillance tapes...and I knew you and I were the only ones outside the cops who saw those."

"What else did the Sheriff tell you?"

"That the CHP guys have determined Suzy wasn't involved in Gunther's drug operation." She does such a roll that I'm afraid her eyes will stick at an odd angle. "Duh, sometimes those state and fed people have a huge blind spot."

"I wish they'd give locals more credit, true. They have kind of a thankless job, though, coming in and not knowing the players. Everybody is a suspect. What's next?"

She grunts. "The part I don't like. Waiting. They got a warrant for the corporation yard, the truck, the tool box and what tools they find."

"How about the guy's house? Where does he live...and what's his name?"

"Well, here's another item that makes my day. They won't tell me. He's just a Person of Interest right now, not a suspect so they're not releasing a lot of information."

Clarice hauls off and kicks the side of my desk. Then remembers she has on sandals as she grimaces and sucks her breath in, "Oh, crap...owww" echoes through my office. Many of the reporters are out on stories so not a lot of heads pop up from the cubicles like prairie dogs at the sound.

"Rats, bad words." She's gotten a grip and realizes where she is. "That hurts like a SOB. I think I broke my toe!"

I stifle a laugh, tell her to sit down and elevate her foot. I make it to the breakroom for ice before I let the laugh out. She's probably hurting, I doubt anything's broken but it's vintage Clarice, kicking a steel object while wearing sandals.

Before I put the plastic bag of ice cubes on her foot, I take a look. She can move the foot and the toe so no broken bones but she'll have a doozy of a bruise for a few days.

The initial pain must have eased off because she says, "I'll just hobble to my desk and write this up." She evens manages a slight grin. "Let's hope the warrant nets something so they can arrest the guy before we have to go to press."

Clarice has the luck of the angels on her side. The Sheriff calls me at seven-thirty to tell me they have a suspect in custody for the two murders in Freeland. It's a perfunctory call, but enough to get Clarice tearing out as fast as her gimp foot allows.

I stick around the office, knowing she'll have some story for page one. She's back by eight-thirty and at her computer. I read over her shoulder.

Kevin Parshelton, fifty-five, employee of Earth/Search and resident of an unincorporated area south of Monroe, has been arrested on two counts of murder and fifteen counts of theft.

The warrant served at Parshelton's house recovered a large wrench with traces of blood as well as a storage shed filled with copper wire, tools, aluminum pipe, stainless steel and diamond drill bits and a Bobcat with two small holes for the screws that held the state property tag on.

Clarice includes a quote from Sheriff Jim Dodson. "Deputies have confiscated Parshelton's computer and will be looking for those websites where he sold the stolen goods."

After she's filed the story, I've read it and it's in the hands of the copyeditors, we take off for a glass of wine at TJ's in the next block. We sit in a booth so she can keep her foot up. She says it's feeling better, even though it's an interesting shade of purple.

We both take sips of wine then look at each other.

"Man, this ends with a whimper." She scrunches up her face. "We had something that could have gone in fourteen different directions. I was personally rooting for some right-wing conspiracy group who was livid at the idea of eminent domain."

"Right. Like something like that is going to fall into our lap, Clarice. We're the Monroe *Press*, not the New York *Times*." I take another sip. "I was hoping for some grass-roots eco-terrorism movement angry over the tunnels."

"Other people get all the good stuff," she says. "I told you this might turn out like our couch murderers, just scum arguing over drug deals. Although," she lights up a bit, "this had an interesting twist with the thefts. I never would have thought to steal tools and equipment from a construction site. How do you fence it? Your local 'Call 1-800 for tons of wire'?"

We look at each other and spit a mouthful of wine out as we both laugh.

CHAPTER FORTY-FOUR

Clarice is happy.

Sheriff Jim Dodson is happy.

The CHP guys have turned all their Gunther information over to the DEA and gone away so they're happy.

I went down to Santa Barbara for Heather' graduation so I'm happy.

Heather is sending out invitations to her house-warming and new-job party so she's happy.

And making me more than happy, Phil comes over for a quick trip. We're going to Monterey in a week, but he says he doesn't want to wait that long to see me. He showed up this morning and will leave tomorrow. We spend a couple of incredible hours in my bedroom then he takes off to buy food and wine for dinner.

Phil's not the quick-glass-of-wine-at-TJs kind of person so his shopping trip is running long. When he kisses me good-bye, he runs his hand over my hair and pulls me into him. "I'm happy I decided to come over this morning. I was craving you too much."

Craving is a good word for Phil. I can tuck him away in a part of my mind and heart when the adrenaline is running, but he's never gone from me. When he's near, I have a craving for touching him. Brushing against his arm, tucking my hand in his, laying my head on his chest all make me shiver with happiness...plus anticipation. He's the best lover I've ever had and there's no such thing as too much.

He's still away when I go out in the side yard to cut some roses for the dinner table. Despite the heat and lack of water, the bushes are in full summer bloom with a strong scent. I'm bending over to smell when I hear the gate shut and footsteps.

"Phil?"

"No, not your lover, you whore of Babylon."

I whirl around and look at a young man I've never seen before. He's big and he's angry and he has something that looks like a bag of rocks in his hand.

He reaches in the bag and quick as a rattlesnake throws a stone that hits my temple. I recoil, trip and sit down suddenly. He reaches in his bag again and whips another rock at me. This one hits my shoulder, knocks me sideways and before I can take a breath, another stone hits my side with such force and pain I think it broke a rib.

Who is this guy? I don't know him. Why is he throwing rocks at me? As another stone hits my hip, my brain explodes with understanding. This is the vandal who burnt Gwen's lawn and he's planning to stone me to death.

"You belong to the Harvest of Praise, don't you? You burnt 666 into my reporter's lawn."

He has another stone in his hand. He tosses it in his hand as he watches me and I see it's a river rock, worn down smooth. Tremendous weight but no jagged edges.

"I did. When I first joined Harvest of Praise I thought I found a church for me. A church that went back to the roots. The first pastor preached cleaning your own house to show the Lord your goodness."

He shook his head and the madness in his eyes dimmed with sadness. "Then they started all this new stuff. Dances for boys and girls, women attending services in pants and shorts, rock musicians at the altar. It's an abomination and your newspaper abets it. Letting the church leaders tell everyone how they want to turn it into a spectacle, an event...entertainment!" A string of spittle forms at the corner of his mouth.

I've seen some crazies in my time, but the venom in this kid's demeanor scares me. I scuttle back but the pain in my ribs stops me. It's all I can do to keep from screaming.

Screaming? The neighbors might hear! Mac might start a barking frenzy!

As I open my mouth and a scream starts, he's on me, kneeling on my aching chest and slamming a hand across my mouth. I can't draw a breath. Panicky, I flail around the ground hoping to find something, maybe one of his rocks. What my hand hits is my Corona pruning shears. Not pointed but spring-loaded and razor-sharp.

I grab them, aim for the hand across my mouth. Miss any fingers but manage to get a piece of the fleshy edge of his hand and snip.

Nothing happens. Then he lets out his own scream and jerks his hand back.

"You bitch! You'll pay for this!" He reaches for a large rock, probably planning to smash it into my skull but is knocked off me by a big black furry shape.

Mac? How did he get out? The kid is screaming unintelligible strings of nonsense and hitting out at a couple of men trying to restrain him. Then there are more people in the yard and I hear the crackling of a police radio.

I try to suck in great gasps of air, open my eyes and Phil is leaning over me.

"Are you alright? Did he knock you unconscious? How badly are you hurt?"

My finger on his lips stops the stream of questions. "I think I'm OK. I don't know if anything's broken...maybe some ribs. My chest hurts where he was kneeling on me and I can't take a deep breath."

The face of a city cop looms up. "The paramedics are on the way Ms. Hobbes and we have your attacker."

How does he know my name? I don't think he's a cop I know. I close my eyes for what I think is a second to run though familiar faces, then feel myself being lifted.

On a gurney, loaded into the ambulance, Phil at my side, an IV started. Haven't we done this before? In the ER, they cut off my top, shoot some painkiller into my IV feed, wheel in some machine. By this time I'm woozy and drifting into and out, then I hear a beloved voice.

"Mom? What happened?"

Heather's here and this time she's staying. I hear her tell someone that she's an RN in the trauma unit at UC Davis. Even with oxygen I'm still not breathing well but a big bubble of pride forms in my chest. I have a smile as the painkiller hits.

People are talking quietly and machines are beeping. I'm not sure where I am and don't care as I float, then someone bumps my bed and I'm awake.

"Oops, sorry. You're one of my first trauma patients and I shouldn't do that!" Heather lays a hand on my arm. "Did I hurt you?"

It's too much effort to smile again so I whisper "No" and I'm gone.

Next time I come awake, it all comes back. I try to roll to my side to touch Phil and let out a grunt as pain hits.

Both he and Heather are there instantly. "Don't try to move too much, Mom. You do have two broken ribs." Heather checks my IV, a nervy thing to do from someone whose diapers I changed.

Phil notices my skeptical glance and laughs. "She *is* a nurse, you know. A big help with your information in the ER."

I look around and realize I'm not in the ER now. Heather says, "They admitted you overnight for observation. You were out of it last night, but they're releasing you today. You can probably go home in a couple of hours. I have to go to work tonight. Phil is going to stay for a day or so."

Phil's playing nurse now? I look at him. Best looking nurse I've ever had. He gives a Gallic shrug and grins. "Told the paper I'm working remote this week. I want to know you're well for next weekend in Monterey."

CHAPTER FORTY-FIVE

I'm home. Phil's nursing me, which mostly consists of him telling me to stay in bed.

He does cook, something I didn't know. When I visit him in the city, we go out for meals or he brings home deli. I discover he makes whisper-light omelets, Béarnaise sauce for the deep pink filet steaks, a mean Salad Nicoise and of course French Roast coffee, strong.

He's set up the spare bedroom as an office and I hear him on the phone and typing away.

"Do you write that much every day?" I ask him as he wanders in for more coffee. By the third day I'm downstairs at my laptop in the family room.

He gives me a blank stare. Is this question too hard? Then he shakes himself and comes back from wherever he's been. "No. Well, yes. Sometimes."

"That's a definitive answer. Which is it?"

"I'm not always working on stories for the *Times*. I'm putting together a book proposal."

"Ahhh, another book on Gothic Revival?"

"Not exactly. I'm still researching to pin it down but I don't talk about it much. Don't want to jinx it."

As a "Don't interfere" message goes, this is polite so I go back to my own email.

There was a big buzz on Monday after my day in the hospital. Get well wishes from the staff, a note from HR at the *Press* reminding me about sick leave policies and if I was out for more than three days I had to apply for short-term disability and get a note from my doctor to return to work. I send an answer back reminding them this was a work-related injury and they're silent while they check it out.

I also had visitors. Clarice came and filled me in on the Delta doings. Gunther's trial is set for six months down the line, Kevin Parshelton is arraigned on two counts of first-degree murder and fifteen counts of grand theft. He's in jail on a no-bail status.

The best news is that Suzy Mohre is back home. Her neighbors cleaned her house and Mark Cruz checks on her several times a day. He's even taken over her garden and put in late crops for her. When Clarice tells me this, there's a glint in her eye.

"You think?" I ask.

She nods. "I think."

Gwen stops by to tell me a delegation from Harvest of Praise has volunteered to repair any additional damage caused by the fire, including landscaping services. "I've always wanted to have a planned yard, but with both of us busy and Gil gone such much it didn't happen." She grins. "A beautiful yard and a husband at home. Life's good!"

Art from the Chamber calls to tell me that the family of the young man, whose name is Jonah, has withdrawn from church membership and may be moving.

A nice visitor comes one evening to have wine with us...and brings a friend. Jim Dodson shows up with Clarice, although she's already filled me in on work.

I finally have an audience to ask what happened the day I was attacked. Well, I know who it was and why he was there, but how did Phil show up with the cops at his heels?

"I'd gone out to the car for the last bag of groceries when your next-door neighbor came over to say hi." Phil's one of those people who have a natural ability to chat anyone up. "We heard the scream, dropped everything and ran to the back. As soon as I slid the door open, Mac was out like a dervish. Your neighbor called 911 and both of us grabbed the kid off you and held him 'til the cops got here. You must be on speed-dial or something with the dispatchers. It wasn't two minutes before the first cop was there."

Phil and Dodson exchange looks. They've met a few times in the past, usually around some accident I had in the line of duty. Dodson is the person who taught me to shoot and helped me buy a gun, a fact not lost on him.

"So far Amy, you've used an iron and pruning shears to protect yourself." He winks at me. "Have you even picked the gun up? Do you know where it is?"

"Of course I do, it's upstairs in the drawer of my nightstand. I haven't shot it since you took me to the gun range."

"It hasn't seemed to be much help." Now he's grinning.

"True, but should I get a Wild West holster and carry it around? So far, I've been attacked in the kitchen and in my own yard."

Phil clears his throat. "I'm thinking she won't be attacked in her bedroom now, anyway." Three pair of eyes swivel to look at him and he's got a cat-that-ate-the-canary grin.

"At least for the short term," he says. "More wine, anyone?"

CHAPTER FORTY-SIX

Monterey is wonderful.

Riding over in Phil's vintage Porsche was a little rough on my achy ribs but worth it for the fun. The weather's perfect and the cool coming in off the bay makes the valley heat a memory.

The group Phil belongs to has put together a smaller version of the Monterey Motorsports Reunion later in the summer. There are races at the Laguna Seca track and a Concours d'legance of Porsches. I'm still sore and don't move too well with my ribs taped but I want to push myself to make sure Phil enjoys his weekend. He's been a brick, looking after me.

At Laguna Seca, Phil chats with his old SoCal acquaintances and seems to be having a great time, so I'm hesitant to complain. Four hours of smelling high-octane race gas, burning brakes and tires and listening to high-pitched engine roar has me fading, though. Just as I shift in the folding chair to give my ribs a rest he looks over and apology flashes across his face.

"Let's go, Amy. I think you've had enough. We can catch up with these guys at the Concours tomorrow." He gathers up our things and we leave for a rest before dinner.

Phil's booked us into a B and B and made dinner reservations at a small French restaurant in the Cannery Row area. It's heaven to be taken care of, to have someone I trust make the decisions. Lying on the bed in our room, I listen to Phil on the phone. His voice is comforting. I'm not understanding him, then realize he's speaking French.

How did I end up with this lovely man in my life? My mind wanders to a place where we're together all the time and I suddenly know that I've fallen for him. Is this what I wanted?

I'm leery of relationships after Brandon. He was so hurtful that I never meant to get involved again. Phil, though, Phil is so different. He's taking things slowly and carefully, building up my trust in him in tiny, easy steps. When we're together he finds those small things he knows I'll enjoy and brings them to me like a cat sharing his mouse. Proud, but not overwhelming.

It's stunning and a little frightening to understand that I want this man. I want to share with him and laugh with him and work with him and wake up with him and make love with him When he looks over at me he's silent for a moment, says "A bientot" hangs up and stares.

Have I grown an appendage? What's he staring at?

"Amy."

"I'm here."

"You are. And for that I'm everlastingly glad. If a man has a woman look at him like you're looking at me, he knows he's found the one."

This time I lose my breath and it has nothing to do with my ribs. I can feel the moisture gathering in my eyes, then it spills over.

"Don't cry, love, please don't cry. Have I hurt you?" He sits gently on the side of the bed and takes my hand.

I swipe my free hand under my eyes. "You haven't hurt me, these are tears of happiness. I was watching you and realized how much you mean to me. I've fallen for you."

He smiles and pulls me to him. "And I for you, my love."

ACKNOWLEGEMENTS

Writing is a solitary effort, but books require a crowd.

I wouldn't be able to finish a book without my family, Darcy, Matt and the girls; my incredible critique group, Pam Giarrizzo, June Gillam and Linda Townsdin; the members of the Capitol Crimes chapter of Sisters in Crime; beta readers Fredrick Foote, Guy Ogen, Rae James, Susan Williams, Chelsea Carter and Nancy Gurnee; and certainly not without my best-ever copy and proofreader, Beth White, whose eagle eye has saved me from myself too many times to count.

Thank you all for sticking with me during this amazing journey.

ABOUT THE AUTHOR

Michele Drier was born in Santa Cruz, California to a family that migrated west to San Francisco in 1849.

Unfortunately, they never found gold, nor did they buy (and hang onto) any California land.

Her mother named her Michael, after author and actress Blanche Oelrichs, who wrote under the name of Michael Strange. Several months of saying, "Yes, she's a girl. Yes, her name is Michael," and her mother finally caved. She became "Michele." Her maternal grandmother belonged to a writing club in San Francisco in the early part of the 20th century and wrote poems and jingles—one of which won her a travel trailer during the Depression.

Michele has lived in San Francisco, the Bay Area, the Central Valley, the Sierra, Southern California and the North Coast.

Her first career was in journalism, and she spent seven years as a staff writer with the San Jose Mercury-News. After returning to school to work on a master's, she fell into a second career, as a non-profit administrator.

She's spent time as a reporter and editor for daily papers including twelve years in management, and was the city, metro and executive editor for daily newspapers in California's Central Valley. During this stint, she judged the

California Newspaper Publishers' Association Better Newspapers competition and won two awards for directing Investigative/Enterprise stories.

Besides writing the Amy Hobbes Newspaper Mysteries, Michele also writes *The Kandesky Vampire Chronicles*, a paranormal romance series. The series was awarded best paranormal vampire series of 2014 from the reviewers of the Paranormal Romance Guild, Book Eight, *SNAP: All that Jazz*, was named the Best Paranormal vampire book of 2014 and Book Nine, SNAP: I, Vampire, was published in 2016.

She's a member of the Society of California Pioneers and Sisters in Crime and lives in Northern California with a cat, skunks, wild turkeys and opossums. Only the cat gets to come in the house, though others try.

Michele loves to hear from readers. Send her an email at mjdrier@gmail.com and if you've enjoyed Delta for Death, please leave a review.

62002900R00161

Made in the USA
Charleston, SC
30 September 2016